# Lei Stand Melodies of the Isles

MATTHEW KRAUS

ISBN: 978-1-964462-42-4 (sc)
ISBN: 978-1-964462-43-1 (e)

Rev. date: 07/08/2024

# Part I

vening and day were fading, it was normal for everyone, and the sky's light blended into the night. The blending in with night lights was hardly perceivable as the natural sunset light pervaded.

It's Hawaii (Oahu).

In the evening, the day was partly cloudy, and the evening light was fading as normal. It was a very fine evening, and the sunset was actually memorable. One would remember this week's golden sunsets forever as of the song "Lahaina Luna" by Kui Lee, which speaks of the golden sunsets of Lahaina on the island of Maui. Sunset viewing made the viewing events more memorable.

Near the lei stand, sets of gardens to the side, the visitors had parking.

A little bit of that golden sunset elsewhere was surreal. A view was unearthly from the Pali Lookout, looking northeastward as the darkness of night approached, which was so like an unusual, memorable dusk. The cliff drop-off view of the lookout up there is steep, and the cold wind there is usually extra strong. It had been a breezy day, and leaves from trees were about; they were blown away by landscape workmen using power blowers for about thirty minutes in the morning.

Members of a tour group visiting the scenic lookout had stayed in their car for a few minutes in the afternoon as the wind buffeted them before getting out. There was nothing unusual about that. They looked around at the lush green foliage, wandered to the edge of the lookout, and looked nearly straight down the gnarly, rocky precipice and outward.

It was in the late part of the day and was miles across the island's east side to the sea. In the distance was the bay (Kaneohe Bay) and nearby on the mountainside, a trickling waterfall; it had rained hard that morning and had rained for a few days before.

Toward the northwest on the other side of downtown Honolulu, up a ways from the main highways, there are land, well-kept gardens, lunch wagons, hiking trails, small farms, and a lei stand.

The days at the lei venue, as usual, go by. As the morning, once, was turning to afternoon, there was a usual trade breeze. At a little garden park site uplands and westward, a bit from the bustle of town but not too far toward the airport, near to a lei stand were times as usual, including the nearby music of The Sam and Frank Duo.

Sam and Frank had recently returned from the mainland, where they had given a few small concert performances including some of their promotional songs, they were at their best. They had been applauded for their song "Go To Hawaii", and they had been asked to play an encore when they played their song "The Hawaiian Islands", which often served as a bridge to their song "Hawaiian Islands Holiday". As they sang that song, which gave an imaginative portrayal of someone enjoying a visit to the islands, someone was booking their trip to the islands at the sponsoring travel company's temporary desk set up at the concert site. The patrons would enjoy the flight having hotel reservations waiting for them, and a list of things to do after they arrived. Sam and Frank ended the set with their song "Sweet Sunsets".

Sam and Frank were returned, again, from the mainland. Here, the local and Caucasian singer-songwriters sat comfortably in a shaded area on wooden park benches and were finishing tuning their ukuleles. Their usual repertoire included their songs "Waves, Rainbows", "Beautiful Flowers", and a standard. The music being enjoyed by the regular group of friends, interested people, and tourists, who had visited the scenic Pali Lookout the day before, was with intermittent comments between some songs; comments between songs could be extensive.

One of the tourists, a man, commented to Frank, "I heard you sing a few months ago on the mainland, "Hawaiian Islands Holiday", and so I made sure I would come to the islands."

"That's right, Sam added, "We were there."

Firstly, Sam and Frank played the standard song "Pretty Red Hibiscus", a Johnny Noble song. They occasionally sang it. Afterward, Sam addressed the small audience.

Sam disclosed, "We have recorded this song, and it is available on a CD recording."

"Yes," Frank added.

Sam continued, "Our recording it again is a possibility."

Frank said, "We play some originals."There was some applause.

Sam said, "Thank you."

Before they went on to play more songs, first, their own, Sam set out a treasured, small woven coconut frond basket for those who would contribute money to their entertaining effort. There were soon some small change donations and a few dollar bills.

Frank and Sam were playing their melodies.

Sam announced, "And now we're gonna sing our own, "Beautiful Flowers".

They sang it and then sang their next song, an original.

Sam announced, "This song is "Flowers in Wind"." And then, after a few moments, the introduction was heard.

Frank imparted, "There's aloha to you."

They played and sang their songs "Flowers" and "Vacation Hawaii", which was one of their promotional melodies, and a cover of "Aloha 'Oe" by Queen Lydia Lili'uokalani, a favorite standard.

There was a moment of quiet and a breeze as they started their strumming intro to their own song "Valleys, Mountains, Ocean". After the first word, groovy, the song was played over and it finally faded out with that punctuated last word of each verse's ending that everybody liked. Frank and Sam looked at each other and shrugged their shoulders, it was time to do another song.

Some verses were continuing, seemingly to be sung by Frank and Sam. It was heard as the song they sang paused in quiet instrumental interludes between the verses so well; it was performed so that those there could enjoy. It was applauded. It was a quick side in addition to the sound of the song that Frank and Sam played; which was with an ongoing continuum verse to verse lyric.

Another tune was soon being heard, and then there was a pause between the songs. The tune took the listener into the appreciation of surf waves, water, and seawater, which was a nearly a right-there experience and one that attracted a look from afar; i.e. the lei stand people. The song had a mellow wave sound and was appreciated by the regular listeners there as a provocative approach to surf songs. Frank and Sam were happy they could continue singing their songs and they did. The short set was finished and there were impromptu comments.

Sam said, "Tremendous sights, monstrous surf, prodigious valleys, astonishing surroundings."

Frank added, "In song."

As they put their ukuleles in the ukulele cases it was quiet for a few moments. Those with good hearing could hear the surf breaking in the distance.

The first person in the audience on the first bench was smiling. They commented, "Isn't it a nice view? Monstrous waves of the ocean are rolling onto the land this cool day?"

Frank replied, "Yes there is a nice sound."

They were happy and well-satisfied with their well-seasoned music.

Frank said, "We will play this next song, "Waves, Rainbows". It's one of our best, and then we may take requests."

People were restless; especially those on the second bench.

Someone commented, "Hey, look, a rainbow."

There was a pause as almost everyone looked in the direction of an extraordinarily bright rainbow fairly close by.

The lei stand people on the street noticed it. An island simplicity was of June Nani and family, average people. Auntie June Nani, who ran the lei venue, was looking for a rainbow for a moment and had earlier picked some white ginger flowers from a neighbor's garden; her picking flowers was with permission and had not taken a long time.

Mack, who was a relative, had just dropped by and was talking, and listening to the songs by the music duo. He came by the lei stand and saw June Nani, who was glad her nephew had come. He had bicycled there from his home, he had come from downtown, taking mostly back streets and then walking his bicycle, pedaling up a rise to the lei stand. He lives about five miles from June Nani's house and had often come to the lei stand.

Mack has time to hold occasional other jobs. He is outdoors and had been doing side work just that afternoon. He was in the June Nani family.

Gladly, Mack would take a job from June Nani. For twenty dollars, he would wash her car, and he'd also enjoy a day by her lei stand where, nearby, he might pick some fruit. If he had brought some fresh, white ginger, he would be given fifty dollars.

Sam and Frank take a breather and rest in the cool of the other side of the parking lot, there were park benches, and they had a good sit. There was virtually no car traffic then, but it wasn't long until a tour group car pulled up.

A tour group visiting the lei stand was glad to talk to someone.

The tour guide commented, "That sky, I think it might be okay today, no rain." The tour guide was talking to the group. Mack, who was occasionally stopping by there, was standing by listening.

The tour guide/driver said, "I know you; you're that pineapple-picking guy. They say we look alike."

"I think so," replied Mack. "I think someone said that?"

The tour guide continued, "Ya, we look similar."

Trade winds were blowing. It's an island, not too big. Lots of paths can and do sometimes most unexpectedly cross, and people can and do become localized to a part of the island.

Many visitors, usually with a tour group, whose tour included going to June Nani's Leis, watched the evening skylight blending into the night as scheduled.

The night skylight and the city lights were illuminating. Skylight and sunset are, for some, the number one ambiance that people many times get into to regularly enjoy watching. Especially nice sunsets were often from the seaside, mostly west-facing.

It was early afternoon.

They played songs. Sam commented about the clouds.

Sam said, "Often, we may see the sky, perhaps paying more attention to the ocean and its many changes daily."

Frank added, "The remnants of a tropical storm, the distant clouds are hardly noticeable. One storm had passed by and dwindled to remnants. Some darker lower clouds of a storm were heavier with rainwater from it, and breaking apart upwind a few hundred miles."

It seemed to remind everyone how good the weather was. They were lucky they were there since impacts such as tropical storms were rather rare.

Sam and Frank tuned up their ukuleles and played a standard, the Harry Owens song "Sweet Leilani", which includes a mention of the sky's jealousy. After the song, they looked each other in the eye for a moment.

Sam said, "Can you imagine the sky's jealousy?"

Frank replied, "Tropic skies."

Sam added, "OK with me."

Sam and Frank often wore aloha shirts with red hibiscus flowers and a background of yellow edging against a blue, wavy background.

Two hibiscus blossoms were imaged on an aloha shirt worn by tourists lingering and enjoying watching the ukulele players sing. The fully expanded blooms of red and yellow hibiscus flowers on a pale blue background are a popular image on many aloha shirts and muumuus. Some visitors would find the nearby hedge of gorgeous hibiscus flowers matching their dress clothes.

One man was heard to say, "I am fascinated by this aloha shirt and aloha wear style. They say it's acceptable, equivalent to wearing a business suit."

Sam replied, "Most times, it is."

Frank added, "Always."

Sam commented, "I like that song."

A group of about seven visitors sat on benches near the parking lot in sight of the flower vendors' main vendor, who was in aloha attire; a flower print muumuu, plus her hat had a feather hatband and had two hibiscus blooms in it on the left side, the flowers being there leftward were signifying the bearer was romantically engaged. Feathered hat bands were a traditional art form, and June Nani had some for sale.

The songsters were playing near a little garden, which with three aloe plants with full blooms of orange flowers on a single vertical shoot that was fresh, was touching. The little garden was somewhat typical of a roadside or trailside garden, possibly to be like some home gardens here and there about the island. With four papaya trees bearing fruit near its face by the road, they were wild and shabby; back in the garden; there was an ohia tree with lehua blossoms. The ohia tree was a little unusual.

Outside the entrance of the nearby boulevard, where there are some large spreading trees, a few egret birds could be seen swooping about. How the trees had gotten there was speculation. There were similar trees in another part of the state. Both areas, the miscellaneous garden with the ohia tree, and the large haole ohia trees are near the lei stand and had been a hard work area many years previous. These haole lehua trees, which grew so large, were beautiful, respectful, and had been planted to enhance the beauty of the area. Their flowers were like a lehua blossom of an ohia tree, which are quite red, and were of paler color.

About the lei stand parking lot, a row of five coconut trees grew to a height of about thirty feet and had bunches of coconut on them; a couple of rows of such trees were behind them and grew a little more slender to a dangerous height of maybe a hundred feet, and some others were about the entrance in front of some bougainvillea bushes with purple and red blooms flourished, their thorns ever sharp. A nearby lineup of coconut trees, also, were dwarf and required no climbing to pick the fruit.

The higher trees' brown fruit were drier and, when husked, gave a tasty snack. Sometimes one such coconut could have fallen naturally and be lying about under the tree.

Mack, who had come early this one day, had found one of the brown, dry coconut fruits fallen to the lawn below it. He picked it up and walked to the parking lot, which was empty. He tossed it high as he could, and it came down with a loud thwack; a few times more until the husk was battered enough so he could grab a strand and start pulling the husk off the hard inner shell. That done, a light toss of the hard shell coconut onto the pavement, despite losing some of the milk, old coconut milk being less appreciable than a young coconut; was so he managed to obtain and consume a little of the liquid. Then, after a while of pulling it apart, he found a little bit of the firm, white coconut meat, which was nutritious and hard to pull off of the remaining hard shell. He found a few squarish pieces of the coconut shell with the meat well attached and with one he brushed the remaining husk strands from it. He found by carefully lodging his front teeth about a quarter inch in from a side he could pry off a little piece of the coconut, which when taken this way includes a layer of interface from the shell, which was thin, brown, and offered a little additional flavor and nutrition. These coconut pieces were often pried off with a dining spoon or butter knife. A correct pull of the hard, hardy coconut often was delivering a whole piece of the coconut.

It was still early and he had time to utilize some of the husk now in a handy pile near the place where he sat. He took a few thin strands of the husk and rolled their ends together between his thumb and forefinger and they bound together, then he took three of these now longer strands and braided them. With numerous extended strands, numerous braided pieces were developing and he could braid the braided pieces interweaving them to produce a longer piece. His fingerprints were slightly worn away from numerous times of this art.

Meanwhile, another time later in the morning, near the lei stand tourist groups were coming and going.

"There are plenty of coconuts to see," said a tour driver to a tourist group. "The high trees are older, the ten-foot trees are in a couple of rows, then there is a grove across the parking lot and back a way, and the dwarf coconut trees, too, are lined up close by."

The tour driver had pulled over near a food vendor there and the visitors were all having luau plate lunch refreshments.

It was near the lei stand where June Nani was prepping flowers and leis, several types of strings were in a refrigerated chamber with a glass door. June Nani's beckoning the buyers to enjoy leis was her standard, the leis were nice at the stand; the scent also from flower blooming trees was enchanting as they strolled across well-kept lawns near a large parking lot to where they could sit on benches and listen to the songsters.

A grove of banana trees was growing inside an old chain-link fence in an adjacent garden nearby, which was introducing a small fruit farm, papaya trees were as far back as one could see.The grove has banana trees bearing fruit, and some were local apple bananas, in one cluster were yellow ripe ones, leaning well over the fence. Nearby in a roadside garden, also were some dry land taro plants struggling but not so well-tended.

Sam and Frank were recently finished with a set, it was well into a long summer day, and they weren't packing up to go home. They played some more.

Checking out the sunset becomes one of the pastimes of the evenings. Even Sam and Frank, songsters as they were, took time off and checked the sunset panorama.

At night there were some observations of the sky movement, stars were well-checked.

As sunset time was accompanied by refreshments, and visitors and friends enjoyed the available treats, a usual, slightly different sunset show was on. From one to the next day, the panoramas of sunsets were enjoyed, usually, on sunset-facing shores.

As the years went by there were changes. Sugar cane became a thing of the past.

Some people like to enjoy the gardens and be in the wilderness as life outdoors.

Cars passed, some drove around the parking lot and back to the main drag; the traffic included two police cars. They liked to park there and eat plate lunches from the lunch wagon in the parking lot.

A husked coconut was being opened by someone tapping it around its circumference over and over with a stone or hammer; after which it would surrender two somewhat perfect halves.

Wallace Nottingham, a cautious person and longtime resident of the islands, is often exercising caution in the wilds where he likes a green, fresh air ambiance. He spends time with his friends in the natural ambiance. Wallace is a little pudgy, a little touchy, and has been going forward working a construction job and having been picking pineapple. He is a lei stand regular, checking in often and going on long all-day hikes sometimes from trails thereabouts.

A little shorter than the average person, Wallace has a wife, Anita, not quite as tall as him, who hardly ever comes out with him to the lei venue. She's a really informed gardener. Wallace is happy and typically visits a lei and flower venue that is well-placed and has various hiking trails and gardens nearby.

He has recently read up on the islands from tourist brochures and learned that the islands formed from volcanoes millions of years before. He noticed a view of more recent volcano action on the island of Hawaii in such brochures.

At home, Wallace talks to his wife, Anita.

Wallace explains, "Anita, you know how I like to be at a familiar outside hangout, out down some hiking trails and off the beaten trails."

"Yes," Anita acknowledges, "I have hiked some of those places.

"You've been hiking on the south side lately?"

"Yes," he continues, "and I'm feeling like really getting into it. There is one place by a restored ancient religious site."

She quizzes, "You went to a *heiau?*" *(heiau*- Hawaiian sacred site(s))

"I might go to one," he replies. "Now I am going to the botanical gardens."

"There are nice places to visit," she suggests. "You might want to go and listen to the musicians who usually perform by the lei venue; Sam and Frank there are pretty good."

"Yes, I know of them," he replies. "They often play near the lei venue."

He recounts that he has found out through articles in visitor and tourist magazines as well as occasional newspaper articles, that there are numerous luau and all-you-can-eat places.

"There isn't much about them in tourist magazines," he says, "just stuff like the luaus."

"You should go to the luau, and eat," she said.

There had been volcanic activity as exemplified in craters on the island's south side a million years previous.

"Might hike to one crater," he replied.

Anita replied, "I was telling you, the landscape alludes to a break-off shelf of the island, downward off Molokai slipped into the sea."

Wallace replies, "Ya, that checks out."

She adds, "Yes, good fishing out there."

Wallace said, "Anita, I've been thinking volcanoes could not erupt again here. But on the south side Diamond Head, looks like more recent volcanic activity?"

Anita replied, "That's just some superstitious speculation."

Wallace is soon leaving.

He says, "I'm going today by the lei stand hiking trails. Probably stop by and say hi to June Nani."

"O.k.," Anita said. "And try get the info on volcanic origins. That's interesting."

He left Anita and soon found himself at the lei venue.

June Nani and her family have owned the lei stand and its house lot for generations. June, who is usually there, welcomes visitors and regulars like Fred Langley and his wife, Madeleine.

At the lei stand one day, before Wallace comes, the owner and Fred talk. His wife is pausing by some sprays of orchids in the far corner on a shelf next to some hand-woven coconut frond birds.

Fred said, "Wallace, is a friend of mine."

Madeleine replied, "He leases. And he also comes and visits these lei stands. He lives on this side of the lookout and his place sits well before the botanical gardens."

Fred adds, "Not under the side of a valley wall, no loose boulder to crash down his way."

Madelaine looks at him. Fred and Madeleine Langley meet Wallace, who is energetic and outgoing. Wallace knows the Langleys are long-time island residents. Fred is retired successfully and Madeleine, his stately wife, is well-off.

They are both fairly tall and are on good terms with the lei venue owner, June Nani.

People like June Nani, who is a great host and has a new salesperson who is a relative of hers helping her out this morning. Mack has shown up and she as usual puts him to work. She has a delivery of leis and corsages that he can take care of.

Many visitors enjoy it at June Nani's lei stand, she works at keeping the flowers fresh and presentable and often sells ladies' corsages and other flowers, usually in leis. She is at times standing around looking at the nearby gardens or/ and listening to Sam and Frank. And most days, they are enjoying the evening sunset and the clouds passing by with an occasional rainbow.

The flower lei stand business is good for June Nani, it's a joy for June, and goes back many generations; she is proud to always have fresh flowers.

The modern life of the area is with many people and includes local people servicing the venues.

Some visitors from abroad come to visit the island, a crowd of Asians visit; and June Nani's lei stand is swamped with customers. Some buy flowers, and with their others, they sit on benches and listen to performances nearby by Sam and Frank.

A regular group of people comes around to the flower vending site at a location a ways from the airport but not too far in the uplands thereabouts.

Many of the people are listening to Sam and Frank. Some others come just to visit gardens or hike out on a trail.

Madeleine has browsed an extended public access garden that has maintained trails through it where kukui trees grew; many kukui nuts were lying about under the trees.

At June Nani's home, lei-stranding parties could be happening. Even at the lei stand site, sometimes baskets of flowers spread on blankets could be seen stranding leis.

At the lei venue area, a nearby parking lot on the other side faces a botanical garden, there among the lush palm trees and other fruit-bearing trees, patrons come and enjoy music and pause awhile.

The lei venue company has an office near a few city blocks to the southwest.

The family had gone with an order that had allowed them to present business into the early evening. Auntie June Nani was once named one of the ten best businesswomen in a newspaper's annual poll, which was keeping to the tradition of the newspaper's attention to upcoming businesses.

Days passed where it usually rained, and occasional drizzles might come and go, especially in the fall.

A thunderstorm nearby might go away from there at times. Perhaps as the thunderstorm went northward, fringing on the mountaintops, it would be just an empty sky where cloud edges might display some flashes of lightning.

It looked like it might rain hard, then dissipate at a high pass, from which one could see the distant seashores.

In the sense of flower leis, some draped around someone's shoulders abounded around and at the lei stand. What had once been a small residential cabin storage shed, it had been renovated into a nice, modern lei venue.

At June Nani's residence, which was several blocks from the last end of the parking lot, there were stores of flowers waiting to be strewn. Several blocks further from some nearby public access garden that had some picnic tables, there were usual groves of flower trees offering their odors of wonder. June Nani and her family and employee friends worked some out of her home.

She often said to the visitors, "You're fine."

The regulars at the June Nani family had often visited the lei stand. It was a last and stopping place where many leis were being strung or stored.

Wallace visited the lei stand and then went to the garden, where others visited. Madeline Landley strolled about quite lovely by a bamboo grove holding onto its own ground. There, with some sparse grasses about, it allows them space about its base.

Then is sometimes the duo, playing ukulele and singing.

Madeline often browses around this area and can sometimes be found there; she sits on one of a bunch of park benches and listens to the singers, who are young men artists of the area.

Wallace has hiked to a spot at the heights of a familiar favorite mountain lookout not too far from a beach site lookout. He likes to look out from heights.

The presence of perpetual rainbows, like clouds and rain, was prevalent and noted in books on other islands, which also depicted the scene as a foreground of lower land areas. He enjoyed some of these.

Why Wallace, an island person, likes to go from the islands from time to time is standard. He typically visits the mainland to visit his friends or relatives out west. There, he is reminded of his island landscapes as visiting his friends lets him have a perspective change, for example, at an off-road park or side road pine tree stretch. This does go long distances, but he returns to his home.

After a visit, with delays, he comes to the end of his off-island venture.

He had gone to the mainland for two months between summer and spring three years before. After he returned, he noticed the rainy season had gone a little into the dry season this year. Another year he really didn't notice that rainy-dry season start and finish and got more into the four seasons.

Many normal island people don't get off the island that much; some don't even get a move to a different area over many years. The considered desire to leave the islands, island fever, is not about to happen to these people. Somehow, being located in a small area for a long time grows on one, and they persist to stay in a local area. They get used to its variations, and they are there through changes in everything from climate to pricing of items in stores.

Wallace is usually staying in homeland foliage, it's a highlands area not far from downtown Honolulu, but he goes to the beach regularly and hikes about those areas.

Wallace has found returning from a walk by well-known beach's sand bars; he is at a home of seashells, he has even, on occasion, picked up abandoned beach towels someone has left, washed them, and given some away. He looked around at sunset this time and saw a crowd leaving the beach, and after a walk-around, he noticed there was some abandoned property.

Another beachcomber was collecting coins using a metal detector. The faint blue sky toward the end of the island late on a nice day beckoned him to look at it. From the wind and himself taking a closer look at the beach towel, he found a roll of twenty-dollar bills in the beach towel folds.

At the end of the daytime, previously, friends had found him picking up seashells or anything of interest from a beach.

Wallace and his wife went out that weekend for dinner; they had deluxe plate lunches at their favorite diner, which was in the suburban highlands near where he lived.

People come and usually dare to overlook the sea from up close on the steep mountainside at the lookout.

Wallace hikes to nearby deep valleys to find a different view of the sea. Afterward, he visits a telephone booth and calls his wife. By then, it is often mid-morning.

This one time Wallace came he looked over a few of the orchid leis at the lei stand. There, the mixed orchid leis, white carnation leis, and orchid-carnation leis inspired his pastime. An orchid corsage and other flowers were on display.

He shops. And as he returns a few flowers, plumeria, and gardenia blooms to the holders they had been sitting in, vases with water in them, he looks to the venue owner and personal friend. June Nani was looking after the lace vase settings and selling them to visitors.

Wallace found time to hike his way through a hardly used trail to a waterfall not too far away.

Coincidentally at this same time, some airline passengers, and visitors en route to the islands were happy to look at the distant pastel sky and thunderclouds.

After the plane landing, they check in to their respective hotels, rest before dining, and take in a show or performance at a club.

On a big stage, performers are set to perform.

The visitors come to buy flowers and leis along with local people

Many events come and go, like school graduations, departing and arriving and marriage wearing a lei. This is where lei-wearing is normal. More permanent leis of shells and seeds are sometimes accompanying the flower leis. The leis are somewhat adopted into the traditions.

Narratives and legends of their time most often included stories of the leis.

Sometimes, at Auntie June Nani's residence, a narrative session goes on. There was a traditional story going on to oral history, which is going very far back, several generations. Then the narrative could go to who's been born recently, who had gotten married, how the children are doing, and at the end of the talk, it got to historical events.

A really intense, more accurate statement could not be found. Taking the form of hula and chanting stories were interwoven.

Sometimes other family people filled in for children at the lei stand.Wallace was loosely adopted there and he and the lei seller often enjoyed the usually soft singing of Frank and Sam in the distance from the lei stand.

As Frank and Sam sang their song "Grandeur of Flowers", once again; one of their earliest original songs, visitors and friends listened from nearby benches. Frank and Sam hummed the song, then sang it softly. It worked really well for them, giving it a feeling.

Wallace found his way to the hike to a spot high up overlooking the sea.On many occasions, he would come back and describe the view to his friends at the apartment where he lived.

After June counts her money when opening, the songsters sing on for a while.

June said, "A while more, and someone comes and asks for a hibiscus bud."

She saw Wallace, handed him a small bag of fresh hibiscus buds from her for-sale collection, and waited.

"Thank you," Wallace said. "I appreciate your getting these for me." He was counting out twelve dollars.

Wallace, who had been to a takeout restaurant earlier, had some hot tea in a thermos with the lid on it. He quickly put the thermos lid back on with the hibiscus bud in the hot tea.

After several moments he drank a little of the tea, which seemed to give him a slight mellowing out, and he relaxed.

"Thank you, June Nani," he said, "this is one cool tea."

"I know," she replied. "I have it every Sunday morning at a farmer's market right by the highway."

After a while, he quickly browsed the leis and other items at the lei stand. Once, as he moved toward the fresh cut flowers, including hibiscus, his sight latched onto eight yellow-purple plumeria leis, hanging ready to be tied, and some flowers blooming sitting in a pretty glass case next to a red hibiscus flower where sprigs of fern reached out.

Some of the hibiscuses had come from a hibiscus hedge in June's front yard, and some had been gathered from an office building's yard across the street.

"Do not just look at them," suggested June Nani.

Wallace answered, "Yes, they're fine. I was just checking their thickness, their aroma strength, and their texture."

June Nani looked at him again with approval and hoped he would buy some more leis and flowers.

If Wallace had been roaming a dense mountain trail, it was not unusual if he had been up to find flowers at the top of the waterfall; he would bring some back. All that he could say was, "This also gives one a nice distant view of the sea."

Wallace came back and looked around for his friends Fred and Madeline Landley.

Another one of the Langley's friends was Marty Chadwick, a friendly, outgoing man they had met from a harbor visit, a traveler from a sailboat visiting the islands. He was now a friend of Fred Langley and his wife Madeline; also he had come to meet Wallace, he had met Wallace the week before as they had been beaching at the same beach.

And Marty was now somewhere walking a hiking trail. Another time he was found resting on a park bench about at the nearby parking lot's garden, which was within the allowed vigorous vocal call if one really tried.

June Nani, the sales lady, sells on to the people coming and going; some are there to listen, without it being jazz.

Many are the wonderful flowers and leis Wallace and many others bought there in their daily life.

They, like most islanders, were also holding to their corsages, single flowers, and leis.

The song "Grandeur of Flowers" was beautiful, and quite repetitive, and the melody had many verses. The words worked to evoke a passion for flowers and joy felt by the singers and accompanists when there, and the listener.

It was all so beautiful, and he paused and listened as in the distance the singers were singing the same song.

The songsters often started out singing the standard "Pretty Red Hibiscus" (Johnny Noble). Then, a song, patiently sung, "Grandeur of Flowers", which wove crescendos and various rubatos, could be heard even in the nearby park's natural landscape; it was a thing that brought some visitors, who took on an hour or so hike sometimes.

Frank had some experience with performing on a stage. And Sam was with him in one presentation, one could not tell the difference between their expertise.

Wallace stood around listening soon as the vendor said, "The song and its verses, the next verses come, and other verses would go on in the distance taking the song to its appreciated few of the many flowers and cents."

Frank and Sam sang "Grandeur of Flowers".

As Wallace hiked and found a trail that went deep into a valley, a trail that had once been an unimproved road, it crossed a stream toward the end of the distant scenic valley, was a way to go, a song of flowers rang true,

Often, June Nani had paused in her stringing leis and hung them up, looking aside for when her friend Wallace would be coming back, to purchase some more floral arrangements. The distance between her and the people singing was such that the listener(s) who usually listened to them would barely hear her, at times, quietly singing along.

The one new friend, Marty, came up to her smiling.

He said, "It's up to the landlady to sing."

She replied, "I don't usually sing those songs here."

Marty had been there a half-hour and then would have asked June to sing if another song were not being played by the songsters. If she wasn't fussy about singing and busy selling leis to visitors, she might.

As Sam and Frank proceeded to meet the visitors, waving and motioning to take a seat, Sam's partner Frank spoke.

Frank said, "Listen to the song "Flowers in the Wind". It is a song written by Sam."

They performed the song.

Some new ukuleles were available from under the counter at the lei stand. She was looking and adjusting the price tag, she gave a knowing look.She handed a playing 'ukulele to Marty, which he took with a sign, a wave of his hand to June Nani, to try it out. He quickly strummed it, pressing on the frets up and down the neck and patting its back. It got quiet, and he gave it back to her.

The songsters, Sam and Frank, came to the end of the song with its accompaniment with a nod to the audience. They could see most parts of the parks and trails around the area, and they had noticed when a solo hiker had gone up a trail, and where they emerged from what might be a different trail entrance.

Frank commented, "We're going to tune up a little bit." Sam plucked a string he usually plucked to tune it, really quickly, then he picked out the melody of a new song and started singing it, and Frank came in accompanying the song. Their small, self-based group was appreciated with applause and coins in the basket.

Marty asked, "What's the next song?"

"Flowers," Sam, more the songwriter, answered. And the song rang true as the duo sang it.

Wallace's chosen hiking trail that day was across a rocky stream with cool water, which was cool and drinkable. He drank some of the water before returning to the lei venue.

At the lei venue were groups of visitors passing a trail entrance nearby and going the other way to listen to the duo.

At least they sang on and paused and looked around as some of the visitor people from a tour nearby were coming to the lei stand to look over some leis.

Marty asked, "Does that song, "Flowers In The Wind" go on?"

"Yes it does," Sam answered.

As the tourists were wanting to buy some orchid leis, and she had them, she paused to take care of the business. Afterward, then, the songsters went on enjoying an easy play tune on the ukulele. Frank sang a verse from the song he had in mind, "Flowers in Wind".

At a not-too-distant suburban park area, friends Wallace Nottingham and Fred Langley were exploring a trail through the small, but flourishing park.Fred and Wallace were parked nearby and got out to enjoy the park hike, which they did.

As they were about to hike, they passed their friends, who were going on a longer hike there. Fred and Wallace were having lunch that day as a diminished breeze blew through the pathways of the park; there, their friends were hiking through flowers, and a breeze blew on as they hiked also.

Most of the park's hibiscus flowers had red petals, there were a few white ones. On nearby hibiscus bushes, the hedge of wide-open, blooming red and white flowers bounced, dipped, and poised in the breeze.

"Those flowers have really nice, white petals," declared Fred.

They were soon headed back to the lei stand site, Fred drove slowly by the corner to come to the lei stand site where he parked the car.

At the end of the parking lot, in the distance, the songwriters' voices were heard singing "Flowers in Wind".

Wallace paused to listen.

He was often out looking for a place to hike; he always had borrowed a bag backpack and had a store of food and water in it when he started out on a trail.He walked past a small grove of plum trees to go forward to the mango trees, which were near macadamia nut trees.

Fred said, "I go up the side of a gulch on the switchback trail till I tire and come back."

"Go ahead," said Wallace, "I'll wait here."

Marty and Fred were about the park nearby the urban parks hosting twelve of these large haole lehua trees. They were such immense trees, they seemed to be pretty old.

Also, nearby on a fence, there was a sign on the gate that was to a lot, the lot was so large one couldn't see the house that was back there, and the sign on the gate read, "the world's largest heliconia collection", and below it, a slanted sign was posted with the words (*kapu,* keep out).

They hiked back to the park and their friends where Auntie June Nani is hosting visitors.Fred had once been invited by the residents there at the heliconia farm to come in through the gate and walk inside the estate grounds and look around.

Then, Fred and Wallace did keep out of places like that, finding their resources on the hiking trails that were marked with red ribbons.

After hiking, they were soon back and Wallace was hanging around the lei stand.He stood listening to the singing of Frank and Sam in the distance and was in awe of the collection of flowers that were nearby shading them and the area. Nearby were close trails with some mountain apple trees, which at the time were blooming purple and leaving a purple blossom carpet on the nearby short pathway about and behind the lei stand.

The song they listened to was "Flowers In Wind". It was sung out amid the soft foliage and slowly blowing breezes leaving them wondering if actually sails could be patterned after flower petals.

Marty and Fred were returning to the well-placed lei venue to find not only Wallace was there, but he was doing some shopping.

On the side of a walkway, usually there just singing along and enjoying themselves, were Sam and Frank. Their mid-performance set started with their song "Flowers".

Sam quietly asked Frank, "Shall we do your favorite, "Pretty Red Hibiscus"?"

Frank was thoughtful, he replied, "That Johnny Noble original, what a favorite!"

Sam replied, "Yes!"

Frank added, ""Pretty Red Hibiscus"."

Sam said, "We should do it first, we should always do our outside songs first."

"Okay," Frank replied. "And if we want to do it to start off the next set, okay."

Sam switched on the mic in front of him and leaned up to it. He announced, "This next song is one of our originals, titled simply "Flowers". Frank caught himself real quickly as he was about to introduce, musically, "Pretty Red Hibiscus"; instead of the song he thought they were going to do. It didn't matter to him, he'd just as soon do "Flowers", but in fact, he was letting the song occupy his mind, especially since he would not only be doing the lead solo intro but would sing. The set went well.

Wallace hung around the lei venue.

Wallace said, "She is appreciative of Sam and Frank singing."

He hung out to the side of the lei venue shack. As business for the day was building he was considering a walk down a hiking trail, perhaps to find some fresh fruit, a guava ripe on the tree, a passion fruit ripe on the vine, or a coconut under a tree.

As long as visitors started browsing and looking over the lei stand.

He found some interesting ti plant cuttings that he wanted that were in clumps of fresh ti leaves to be left around them.

Marty kept a distance from the performers, he was just able to hear some of Frank's singing

After a little while, while getting around to the front of the lei venue, Marty was looking over the merchandise, and he stopped.

"Do you like what you see?" asked June Nani.

He answered, "I'm smiling. When can I buy some of the t-shirts to match?"

June Nani replied, "Anytime. These days, I have them so people will come back. It's early, so I want to be certain about getting the fresh ti cuttings. Good, come early tomorrow, I will have t-shirts."

"I'll make a reminder," Marty replied. "I'll come early next time, sometime."

Marty wandered away and around the attractive gardens. He paused to enjoy the fresh air.

He proclaimed, "And if you and yours apply your free will and look around here, if it's up to the distant coconut trees, so tall, to drop a coconut; if it might change your day to a better one, enjoy; breathe, take a few good breaths." No one was around him nor heard his soft voice.

June Nani was getting the shop ready to handle customers. She listened to Frank and Sam sing. She was also watching to meet and talk to Wallace.

Wallace came. She watched him like a hawk and he went on taking bags of leis, feeling them and looking at them, sniffing their fragrance, and putting them back.

She asked, "Are you putting some aside for a big purchase?"

Wallace replied, " I'll take two of the plumeria leis, one orchid lei, and a small orchid corsage for my friend, Madeleine. Madeleine, I'm sure will like this one."

"That's okay with me," said Fred.

Fred Langley, Madeleine's husband, who had appeared nearby, was watching and listening.

"Okay that'll be sixty-five dollars," declared June Nani. "And if you want ti plant cuttings, be here tomorrow, they will be five-fifty each."

He replied, "Okay, I'll be back." Wallace handed Madeleine a packaged lei as he left.

After a little while, June Nani was listening to the singing of Sam and Frank as they progressed the repertoire into the song, "Flowers". She sighed as they sang.

Their singing trailed off as new customers came to look over the flowers.June Nani smiled and they all paused and listened as mynah birds were playing not too far away. The birds had a gentlemanly like attitude.

At the nearby garden benches sat the gentleman singers Frank and Sam.Behind them was, not far from them, an orchid wall. The orchids of the wall were made of cultivated orchid plants hung on trellises that were part of the overall garden outlook, which was provided by a caretaker, who came and worked. He kept it well-trimmed. It was shaped well, looking like a giant clam shell.

Sam and Frank were a couple of good musicians. Seated on one of a group of benches before them, there were, as usual, visitors and tourists. With these songwriters and their melodies, there was often an air of goodwill toward the audience.

For a moment, the first tuning was good, and that is, the strings came to a near-perfect pitch and there was some listening. With a change of the strange sounds they made getting there, Frank started humming his tuning pitches, then he strummed and changed chords.Sam used a relative pitch, tuning all strings from one string that he knew was the correct pitch by hearing it. He tuned until the instrument was all in tune and he was soon all tuned up with Frank.

After a while they went on to sing about waves, leis, rainbows, valleys, mountains, the way birds sang when big waves were breaking, they sang of rain in the valleys, typical hot day beach sands, and flowers; then of the birds, and of the visitors staying on vacations. Those on vacation often say melodies are why they came back; they say that of the songs of the islands. Playing melodies with words is controlling words and ends well.

Frank said, "It is so nice to play in gardens near downtown and uptown."

Sam replied, "Yes, it's a pleasant experience, I just like the green lawns between labeled plant displays."

Frank added, "It's so nice they have all the plants here so well labeled."

Sam replied, "Great for those on a holiday or those with a bent for horticulture."

Frank added, "The islands are great for that holiday."

Sam commented, "It's nice too, off the beaten path trail, all the plants there are treasures. Lookouts near here are great for when this surf is up."

Frank said, "Good to see a set out across the ocean."

Some visitors and acquaintances were looking at their CD sales presentation. One man was looking over the collection.

"Are you near to buying a CD?" Frank asked.

He stopped and looked at him.

Sam added, "It has a lookout over the surf."

The man said, "Yeah, we can go there."

Frank said, "There are lookouts for beach chairs."

Sam added, "That's right.'

The man said, "Sounds right."

Frank said, "Maybe we can go to an up-the-line lookout and park, play some songs, and at the same time look out towards the sea?"

Sam replied, "Blessings for your room with flowers so we can go there in a CD recording."

The man said, "I'll buy a bouquet from June Nani and a CD here."

"I've got a nice CD here," commented Frank.

"We can go there in our next set," added Sam.

Tours for stopping at the beaches and getting to the lei stand for the latest and a seashell or two, which were being sold on display there were doing well. And they did well.

Sam started playing a song and Frank recognized it, "Pretty Red Hibiscus". As he sang, they played the music at the end of each verse.

They accomplished that, which was so appreciated by the crowd.

Frank said, "Then you start playing one of their favorite songs, it's an accomplishment in itself."

Sam said, "Let's do "Waves, Rainbows"."

As the song's slurry introduction was faintly heard nearby, this was where Madeleine had just come out of a hiking trail, she paused there. After hiking on a trail, the song was welcome, so she sat on a bench, and rested.

June Nani commented, "This music is the best of what we have heard from Sam and Frank."

And so Mrs. Langley was comfortable, she sat calmly. After the song, she got up and walked about a quarter-mile. It was a large, long parking lot, a loop, the trail entrance was passed, so she came back to the benches and rested on a bench of a cluster of benches there.The coconut tree grove was in the distance.

A coconut tree nearby gave her some shade.

Frank and Sam noticed she was there and so they kept on playing "Waves, Rainbows".

The song that was being played was being listened to. Visitors were on park benches; and Madeleine enjoyed the moderate music, the musical soft tone was relaxing, and not forceful.

The lei stand was doing good business as Sam and Frank played songs of the flowers, which was heard near the lei stand. There, daily visitors came by to see some of the flowers at the lei stand. They would sing songs including "Waves, Rainbows" one day.

Sam said, "We're doing "Waves, Rainbows" now."

The visitors sat quietly for a moment reveling in the song that they had just heard played. Sam and Frank glanced at the several people sitting nearby listening, and some were quietly applauding. Frank slowly laid his instrument down for a momentary pause as Sam did the same. It wasn't long before picking up their instruments again to play again.

Sam announced another song, "We would like to do a new song."

In the meantime, once again it is getting dark in the suburbs, elsewhere where Fred and Wallace have been hiking a garden. It's Sunday afternoon and they're driving about twenty miles per hour, requiring slowing about five miles per hour before coming to a slow stop and going at a stoplight. A traffic sign nearby showed where parking near the restaurant was. They were talking about having a good time hiking.

Fred said, "I always have a good time hiking with you, Wallace."

Wallace replied, "Well I know where some good, interesting hiking trails are."

Their walk into the vast gardens near where they were parked was rewarding. Having just had mahi-mahi dinners at a restaurant, they finished hiking nearby to the restaurant gardens and prepared to leave to go back to the lei stand. They had just finished their wandering in the whereabouts of a fine garden, and Fred is thinking of Madeleine his wife, she is standing by listening to music and waiting for them, and the takeout dinner of a mahi-mahi plate.

Fred was buying dinner.

He said, "Would dinner from a takeout restaurant be okay?"

Fred had wanted to see the shopping areas near where other restaurants were. So he parked.

Wallace commented, "There, we might have a better deal."

Fred bought a plate lunch to take it back to his wife Madeleine.

After they got situated and had gotten the plate lunch, they headed back.

Madeleine, who is within earshot of the lei stand, is now sitting and resting, still listening to the music. She was thinking of her husband who was gone for an awfully long hour and a half. He'll be back soon, she thought. She's one to wonder, he's bringing me a mahi-mahi plate lunch. He said he would, I hope with some desert. I hope he has found a good take-out restaurant.

Fred and Wallace soon returned after they had finished eating their dinners. The desserts were taken back with them to have at the lei stand with Madeleine at the parking lot's side benches.

They had eaten and left, and the restaurant dining had gotten them to pause. As they finished and went to the car, unlocking the car was a moment, and soon, they were headed back to the garden and lei stand area parking lot. As they got to the lei stand, they passed a few classic archeological sites, and it was an uneventful drive.

The archeological sites, well noted, that they had passed had been thought a mystery of the land, and the roadways around it were lined with beautiful, flowering trees, which was quite memorable.

As light-headed as she was, Madeleine ate the mahi-mahi plate lunch, which was still warm, and had the chocolate pie on the side as Fred took a few bites from his chocolate pie.

The Landleys were together, and just as if they were finishing dining together again, the music started.

Frank and Sam were in the front of a small audience where Madeleine finished eating. She glanced up and over the singers and paused as a rainbow was situated beneath a distant rain cloud and was fading. As a shower was passing by in the distance giving faint, audible thunder, the songsters were tuning their ukuleles again as they found another song to sing.

They played their standards and looked around.

Madeleine, who had finished her lunch, was listening and Fred was now there seated comfortably.

After finishing her mahi-mahi plate, which had rice and coleslaw, she said, "Thank you, Fred."

He went back to daydreaming of hiking by a historic site entrance.

And for a few moments, as the ukulele songs were playing again, Madeleine was daydreaming of back on the hiking trail. Leis were on visitors, new and being worn. Listeners went about thirty yards, a way into the foliage on a trail, and they could still hear the music.

As the duo played, a group from a tour, the group had recently flown to the islands and had come to rest there just as they were taking in the music, were settling down. This was also where Mrs. Langley sat.

The musical entertainment paused. The tour group all enjoyed the music. After the songs paused, they wandered about in the landscaped area of the park as Sam and Frank were taking a break. The music paused, they were relaxed and enjoyed the break before playing music again. They listened to enjoyable entertainment discussions.

The tour guide spoke to his group, "They are taking a break."

Frank said, "Aloha." and rested, turning off their mics.

After a while, they were set to play again. They turned on their mics.

Sam added, "Aloha."

The group there replied, "Aloha."

They played into their song list.

A couple from the tour group, who had been there listening to their songs placed a roll of dollar bills in the basket that they had placed in front of them. These musicians were soon taking a break.

As the group there had been listening to Frank and Sam, Sam introduced, musically, their song, "Valleys, Mountains, Ocean". They paused for a minute before they started playing the song.

There was applause as they finished, it was a fade-out ending.

Frank said, "Mahalo."

"Mahalo," said Sam and Frank, both in unison.

Frank added, " Did you hear the song back there?"

There was some nodding yes in the back of the small crowd.

Frank and Sam were stopped and they looked around, a couple from the group applauded Sam as he applied Frank's solo, it was a moment of rasgueado strumming he had studied up on, he quickly then broke into a pacified tempo.

Sam said, "Wasn't that interesting? But right now, I'm not sure, really sure, if we should call on our song."

The song was sort of a short one, but with the slow tempo, it stretched out. The beautiful melody they played gave it a deep feeling, and with some complicated chords they played, it reminded those listening to be appreciative of their song.

They all were enjoying the moderate breeze slowly happening by. As Frank and the duo were warming up and playing their ukulele tune the trade wind breeze gusted a little.The sound of the breeze on the microphones they had was audible. For a few seconds while the tour group was listening to the tune warm up it was steady.

Meanwhile, a naughty wind gusting drew long pauses.

And in the distance was Wallace there, he and Fred were straining to hear the music.

Nearby, the tune was a happy song and it started off fine.

Again, they played "Valleys, Mountains, Ocean".

Some coins from some purses were given as the music continued to be played by the singer-songwriters. This money given seemed to be toward the song just sung by Frank and Sam. To them, it was a usual stipend.

It was a here-and-now landscape song.

That this was the song they sang was accepted by everyone in the audience, though some who were listening for "Beyond the Reef" (Jack Pitman), were happy to hear "Hawaii Aloha" (Reverend Lorenzo Lyons) and sing or hum along.

It was their song "Oahu Room" Sam and Frank played, after which they paused and had a quiet moment.

They adopted the instrumental bridge of their song "Lookouts For You" to an introduction, which was so well performed by Frank and Sam adding a flair; in the handling of their instruments, Frank held his instrument up by the neck.

At the end of the song, it appealed to the small audience as those there applauded, the instrumental was a quick addition. Aside from handling their instruments and playing to the sound of the song, Frank and Sam played with an ongoing lyric.

In another spoken bridge, Frank commented, "Another tune may still be heard when there is a pause between the songs." And the tune took the listeners into the appreciation of waves and water, the sound of waves breaking, a prerecorded addition being played from a digital recorder up close to the mic, it was a bright side to the experience and attracted a close look. The song had a mellow wave sound and was appreciated.

Someone in the audience said, "That's an approach to old songs."

Frank and Sam were happy to continue singing their songs.

The short set finished with members of the audience from two continents applauding. They were smiling in approval.

Sam's tremendous songs, besides including the sounds of monstrous, prodigious surf that violated astonishing surroundings, were applauded. As they had their songs of the local area recorded to CDs, with their instruments in their cases, it was quite quiet for a few moments and the music was for sale.

The first person in the audience commented, "Isn't it a nice view, monstrous waves of the ocean rolling onto the land?"

Sam replied, "A go-to-school day for many local youngsters and a beautiful morning and early afternoon ocean viewing time for visitors and regulars who enjoy it "

Frank added, "Also, a few fishermen."

They saw the crowd there including students who were happy and satisfied with the music.

Wallace, who was often hocking a cassette player or some other such thing had come out of a hiking trail exploring along a shore precipice and hiking along a trail near the edge of a lookout that was a relaxing hangout time were adventures employed by many residents.

There had been an air raid siren test this one day.

Frank asked his audience, "Did your group eventually return to their homeland by air?"

Sam added, "After, a beautiful view of your friends, an aircraft and cloud formations, and distant mountain tops in the foreground you start back into the appreciation of the view."

Meanwhile, Mack was talking to one of her other sometimes pineapple-picking relatives.

She said, "Mack, I see you came to visit here?"

"Yes, I often do," he replied.

"Are you still working in the pineapple fields?" The lady pineapple picker asked.

"Yes," Mack replied, "Almost every day."

A visitor guide commented, "Sometimes they need your help up there packing pineapples."

The visitor was from an official pineapple store and had worked boxing pineapples for visitor purchase as well as, in special boxes, mail orders.

It was the middle of the day, an episode of pineapple packing one week, and actually picking pineapples the next week was what Mack was into.

"Maybe I will come," Mack said.

As June Nani looked at him, she went on to a customer.

The customer said, "I am buying over a hundred dollars worth of flowers, plants, ti-plant cuttings, sugarcane, sugarcane cuttings, and other stuff. I like those coconut frond birds and hats."

June replied, "They're not as cheap as you might think."

The customer paid her and June said, "Thanks."

At the lei stand sometimes-there relative, Mack, had walked around the area passing by some hiking trails' entrances, and then returned to the lei venue before heading to his home, about fifteen minutes ride away.

Wallace had come and stopped by before embarking on a trail that could get him an outstanding overview of a valley to the sea.

He said, "I come about to see the parking lot from time to time." He had found the hiking excursions before, and he went on one he had spotted a nearby lightning storm and rainbow there before. And as a well-placed trail, it went about a fruitful hike. Then. on some other hiking trail, he had found some really nice places to look out toward the sea, which is what he was after.

Another time days later, Frank and Sam had come to play their music again. Their singing trailed off and new customers were coming to the lei venue when Marty and Fred Langley came by.

Fred said, "I've been there and we're leaving for an afternoon hike."

The hike, which was to a place that is usually shrouded with overgrowth inspired considerations of trail clearing. One trail went left to an exciting lookout, and the other went left from there to return to the lei venue area right about where the songsters, Sam and Frank, played.

On a bench in front of a flower collection, was the entire area a garden if one considers that the well-kept lawn was a garden of some such proportions. In front of the orchid collection tied up to a wiry fence that curved behind the bench where the songsters played were certain ferns that covered the flowery wall, covered with orchids and green plants; that was an ambiance to enjoy. It was the outlay that backed them up and looked like a clam shell.

Marty and Fred were going to the other side of the main road to a parking lot for the suburban ambiance; it had a park-like ambiance. It was like a park that had benches and trails.

In the meantime, Sam and Frank's song playing faded out as it was the hot genre. And Fred and Marty had walked on, driven on, and were at a distant park site. Marty was soon looking afar to a way, to a suburban street arriving at a cul de sac with a vacant lot, which was next to a public right-of-way. So, into a forest reserve that had gone on marked hiking trails, they went. The trails were marked by the state's management system. They were on the outskirts there.

Wallace said, "Ready, set?"

This was but one trail that the hiker may take into the forest reserve.

The other hikers noted Wallace had quickly hiked into the trail. After a while, they were well separated and enjoying their vistas.

Wallace, who had come to enjoy transportation with cycling, had rather than go along on a forest trail, he was closer to the sea, paused at a lookout where waves that usually were breaking precariously were.

Somewhat nearby, a solitary Wallace started walking to a hiking trail.

Frank stands up, stretches his arms, and as Sam was stretching his legs, Frank leaned over to Sam and asked him a question.

Frank asked, "What shall we play next?"

Sam replied, "We'll play our usual."

As usual, it was a long break and they took the full break. It was some time to do some of their songs, and they were debating where to go in their repertoire.

"Aloha," said Frank, "Let's redo songs with aloha."

"I don't know," Frank," Sam added. "I think we're doing the promotional songs."

"Okay, what song shall we sing now?" Frank asked.

"Let's stay with the promotion for a few," Sam replied.

Soon, they were playing and noted that some patrons didn't stay that day.

Sam commented, "Frank, where is everybody?"

Frank replied, "I don't know."

So they played at a moderately brisk pace.it sounded so good they were definitely showcasing some songs.The elements of tourism and traveling between islands were a good choice, "The Isles Holiday" song the best. To show it, this was the day they had a musical repertoire and a song. They saw it was accepted and that was really good. it was interesting to a lot of the people hanging around here.

Frank's playing the melody repeatedly slowly faded down as a signal the song was over, some attendees were leaving, then both Sam and Frank knew it was well done. And the applause told them it was quite okay. They had studio-recorded music for sale on CDs; this was out front for sale and a few people were at their display shopping around. They were, mainly as Sam and Frank went into doing the introduction of their next light-hearted song. They noticed a lot of the visitors were pausing and buying their recorded music, and through the many CDs (compact discs) that were out for sale, and they watched for a few moments.

Mack came to where Sam and Frank were and between songs caught their attention.

Mack broke the silence, "I will gladly watch over your CDs and things. You are going to be glad I do, there are lots of sales you can get."

Sam looked at Frank, and Frank looked at Sam; they both shrugged their shoulders and agreed, nodding affirmatively to let Mack watch over the CD sales.Frank pointed his finger briefly to Sam, meaning you let Mack know.

Sam waved Mack in, and commented, "Mack, we could use some help with the CD's income. I'll pay you thirty dollars a day."

Mack replied, "OK."

Sam added, "Get started right away. We're getting ready to do the next set."

Sam and Frank and relying on their capos to give an alto ukulele accompaniment to their next song, the introduction was long and did the trick. Frank noticed Mack hanging out next to their CDs.

Frank said, "Aloha."

The small audience responded with, "Aloha."

The music went at a moderate pace.Everyone there was enjoying this music, it was another one of those songs they had that parodied the tourist way in a way that was appreciated by the tourist visitors as well as those who catered.And they performed for them. The song was about them. About to hit it into another song, which they did with a start with the second verse, all eyes were on them.

The music went at a moderate pace.Everyone there was enjoying this music, it was another one of those songs they had that parodied the tourist way in a way that was appreciated by the tourist visitors as well as those who catered.And they performed for them a song that was about the many tourists.

There was a pause as they caught their breath.

Satisfied with the enjoyment of listening to the stories and songs of Frank and Sam, the tour group party applauded.

A man asked, "If it was okay, they go away now?"

Sam said, "Surely,"

The man asked, "Do you have another song you want to play now? Are you going to play another song right away?

We are going to go pretty soon, but we don't want to miss your song. We might even extend our stay to listen."

They weren't going at first, but then they looked around at the rest of the small tour group they had come with, who were still listening to the music as it was being played, enjoying the comments of Sam and Frank, which was exciting, and the music which was fading had been in the air. They considered staying to listen to some more songs, when Frank and Sam went into warming up their musical talents with an intro, and they were going into singing one or another of their songs.

Frank looked at Sam, and Sam read his eyes; he looked for a few seconds extra pulling away to the ambiance as usual. Frank wanted to take a break but he wanted to play the song "Waikiki Sand/At Waikiki", which was actually a couple of songs. This had been on their minds to perform for a while, it took a while to do, ten minutes or so.

Many people who were coming again and again to see their friends Sam and Frank, they had come summer after summer, year after year and were bringing family to sit beside them. A family or a friend was a member of their family. Some visitors, who were there for the first time, appreciated the music performance with ten dollars into the basket. Then, one of the men, who had mingled with the tour group, though he was not from the same tour group and hotel, was noted.

He said, "Play those Waikiki songs as a suite ."

Frank and Sam nodded, and started tuning their ukuleles. Sam, when ready, pushed the programmed rhythm for this song, a button on their little battery-powered rhythm assist device that sometimes accompanied them and it got going so they were ready to play the song; they were actually going to do it. They listened to it for a full about thirty seconds as it grew in volume before they started singing the first part of the medley.

They added playing of the vamp, a particular key and chord sequence to use as an introduction and bridge or riff guide. The vamp that they had used included the appropriate rhythm for the song, a particular programmed rhythm machine doing the job there.

A vamp was the custom for many songs they play, at the introduction and between the verses. This was so-so, since their intro was at the finish of the vamp, and they played it again. And it was relaxing. At the end of the vamp, an intro to the song went into the song. And then, with the instrumental melody of the song played as a solo, it was an introduction, they had it arranged there was a crowd-pleasing well-arranged song, the Waikiki Medley; including "Waikiki" (Andy Cummings).

There was a moderate trade breeze gusting about them, as usual, and as usual they were playing outdoors, and as they started out with the introduction, the song seemed to introduce the melody.

Sam introduced the "Waikiki Sand/At Waikiki" song medley while strumming the introduction and refrain over, with Frank adding his accompaniment.

Sam paused and commented, as the music carried the song,

He explained, "This song is our original. Frank actually wrote the "Waikiki Sand" part in one of a series of poems he wrote. He wrote this one song of the poems.

"The series of poems he wrote took over a week of early morning meditations."

"This was several years back," added Frank.

Sam continued, "He was following a free concert at various parks and attended this one at the uplands that connect to this park here.

"Here it is:"

Perhaps partly inspired by the subject, Waikiki, was some of the music; some visitors as well as regulars about the parks and trails often took a fond trip to Waikiki.

As they played the finishing song of a set, a fine refrain and ending seemed to linger. And as the tour group left as it was time for them to go, there were limos with their engines started ready to take them back to a hotel, and some of the people dropped some coins into the upturned basket. Frank tightened his cap.

"Aloha," said Sam, waving as they left.

"Mahalo," added Frank.

Fred Langley and Marty Chadwick were just leaving on a short walk nearby from the lei stand to a not too distant fern forest area, which was nearer to the town side than the ravines often hiked.

The evening twilight was approaching as they returned from their short hike, just coming back from their hike and Fred had wanted to go to Waikiki.

"Let's go to Waikiki for the night?" suggested Fred. "I'll pay for the room."

Marty agreed, "A double room; two twin beds, and I'll ask for a partition."

There was a moment of silence.

Fred replied, "Okay,"

It was late in the day and Fred called his wife Madeleine to say he'd be out all night with Marty.

"We decided to head to Waikiki for the night," he said.

"How exciting," she replied. "I'll see you when you get back."

Then, he and Marty went to downtown Waikiki. They drove around, Fred was driving, and passed several hotels before finding one for the night. They were lucky to find the room on the first try."

They were at a familiar Waikiki hotel. Marty was most familiar with the hotels and Fred had parked the car on the street while Marty took up a conversation with the desk.

That taken care of, as they were, they came to spend the night in the hotel on the eighth floor with a view. Into the night, the night awareness caught Marty, and after Fred had gone to sleep for the night, slipped out the door, down the elevator and out onto the sidewalk to a nearby, all-night convenience store to buy some snacks.

As he was leaving the store, he had a brown paper bag with some chips and juice drinks: a wrapped banana bread, and a packaged piece of cake, *kulolo* poi (sweet taro), also labeled and wrapped in cellophane. And the label read that it was sweetened with cane sugar. Marty paused. As he walked by a bus stop and a lady caught his eye. Had he seen her before, it passed through his mind. She was waiting at a bus stop. He was an old friend, and they spent about an hour there in the midnight hour as the light crowd of nighttime folks swept past and forth by the bus stop bench. This was where there were two benches, they had room to sit on the same bench with their back to the buses.

A late-night bus slowed, and she waved it by.

"Are you going to miss your bus?" he asked.

"Not really," she answered. "I know these buses and there's one or two more."

"Do you want to come up to the room?" he asked.

Marty and his girlfriend had dated and lived together within the last few years, they were compatible; they had some time ago been cohabitating, she had been getting by with some specially dedicated times, and some of their lives were similar.

As he was leaving, he passed the storefront where they had met. He walked up the uncrowded street at one o'clock in the morning and watched as the next bus slowed to take her back to her way. And there were several buses waiting on that one as she was talking to the driver.

Marty and his old girlfriend had revived their friendship at Waikiki. It was in an old-fashioned way, shaking hands on an especially dedicated time in the future to renew their acquaintance. So with this chance meeting, he was with the possibility of getting together with her in the coming weeks. He had proposed to her once in the past, and now, this was the time they might get it together.

As he quietly came to the door of the suite he had with Fred, the thin carpet allowing such quiet walking, he entered. Fred, who was sleeping still, snored a little.

Marty relaxed and went to sleep.

Fred and Marty, who were up at about eight that morning, had a few snacks such as packaged apple pie, canned fruit drink, and potato chips. Fred had to return to meet Madeleine as the noon hour was approaching.

Before arriving back at the rendezvous, Fred and Marty talked.

Fred, who was still tired, asked, "Marty, where have you been besides Waikiki and downtown lately?"

Marty replied, "I've sailed to the mainland, California mostly. Now I stay at the boat harbor there, and on other islands."

Their talk went on and others were coming and walking by the site.

Meanwhile, Wallace, who had come and gone out on a trail for an early morning short hike from the nearby garden park, was coming back.

Wallace, who had spent some hours ascending some highlands with a gulch side, a hardly used trail, slippery in places from an overnight shower, had recently come to view the over-the-trail sight of the distant shoreline. He was relieved to be back, though it was still early and midday.

The famous blue, tropical skies were bringing out some clouds passing by on this partly cloudy sky day. The lei and flower venue nearby was doing steady good business. It was another beautiful day in the islands.

The regulars of the park, lei venue, and entrance to hiking trails had gone from the lei venue and some were elsewhere about the landscaped park. They had been doing their thing in coming and going from there to spend a day off the main roads and enjoy the cool greenery. Some had come regularly for months. The weeks have gone by for some without much notice of a change in the weather or the loads of people visiting. The regulars had often met at the lei stand, the sales side facing the parking lot usually, and some either went for a hike in the uplands nearby forest reserve or took a more winding path that had numerous entrances. As some had gone to a near uplands park fern patch near the forest, there were a few ways if someone wanted to go downtown, a trail that had botanical gardens available was somewhere near a place to have lunch, which wasn't far from the parking lot and lei stand area.

June Nani asked Marty, "Where do you usually stay, Marty?"

Marty answered, "I don't get asked that a lot. Sometimes I work on a sailboat and we anchor nearby to Waikiki, there's a time when it approaches a peer and we can come ashore. But it's easy to access and I like to sleep there."

Marty and Wallace had strolled about and around to listen to Frank and Sam. They had gotten to the lei venue area and waited on the nearby benches for Sam and Frank Duo to start performing again.

There was an old song in the air, Frank and Sam started out in time doing an old standard, "Pretty Red Hibiscus". Listeners were nearby on a large rock that was just right to sit on and was their park bench. The old song was sung and the singers looked at some note papers and went on.

Auntie June Nani, who was nearby there had strolled from her stand when Mack came, was there, humming to the standard. Marty liked the song and noted she hummed it along really well.

About then, Frank and Sam came to sing some of their originals. This was early in the performing day, around lunchtime early into the afternoon singing a few songs. Birds chimed in the distance as the listeners got comfortable watching them sitting just in front of the orchid wall.

The Langleys came and took seats on a nearby, facing bench. June Nani talked to them before returning to her lei stand.

Auntie June Nani coached, "When you sing falsetto, boys, try and hold the high notes a little longer than usual. You just did alright."

Frank and Sam replied in unison, "Okay, Auntie."

"Eh, mahalo, you guys," she added.

Sam commented, "Thank you, Auntie, we'll try that."

"Thank you June," said Fred standing nearby. "They needed that." He patted her shoulder softly a couple of times and she returned to her venue.

June faced Fred and asked him, "You know Fred, I've never asked you this before; I know you're married, but are you gay?"

Fred, an old guy, replied, "No. Not recently."

Wallace, who had finally come around from his hike, was well prepared for a possible strenuous afternoon standing behind the crowded benches to listen to his favorite duo sing. His hike had taken him on to his favorite seashores and now he was glad to relax and listen to Frank and Sam.

It wasn't long, not more than two hours, which wasn't too long when he was dropping off Marty at the lei stand site. Auntie June Nani would be glad to see him.

Fred's wife, Madeleine, was sitting on a park bench with a back and enjoying the nearby work of the Frank and Sam Duo. Mack, too, had just come from talking to June Nani, he had brought some white ginger and been given a fifty-dollar bill. Mack noted Madeleine, mentally, was sitting for a while there. When Fred came Mack was going in that direction and commented.

Mack commented, "I see a nice woman here." He was thinking about what June Nani had told him, and kept walking; he went on.Fred looked at him as he strolled on going off the concrete and right down a path near the heliconia flower farm.

Mack knew where some wild white ginger was, he might get another fifty dollars. They were about a stream near the bottom of a gulch near thistle berries growing wild. He could enjoy a few thistle berries, a drink of the stream, pick some white ginger, and hike to a shortcut to the lei venue before hurrying home.

June Nani, who had strolled away for a while, clapped for the performers; from a distance. She had sung the song as they were singing and before she knew it that singing that was to be done so seriously, was so easily done.

Marty came from the distance of a hiking trail entrance, and from sitting on a park bench, he had walked to the lei venue then, to see June Nani, and to listen to the music.

Since Wallace was there, he was chatting with her, and he was soon with them. He quizzed her on who was the group's inspiration.

Wallace asked, "Did you know the key for that song?"

June Nani answered, "Yes, I had heard it before and for sure, I sang it."

Fred Langley, who was standing behind Marty, had just walked there from June Nani and replied, "They all sell, for sure."

Wallace shifted his weight. He added, "Look. Here comes a car full of tourists. They'll be wanting leis for sure."

"And add to that, they like to chat," Fred added.

As the tourists were from a limo and some were going straight to listen to Sam and Frank, a large, sleek, black car pulled into the parking lot. It made some noise.

"And here comes that guy, Fred, the lawyer," June Nani said.

Mr. J. Thwarton, the driver, a magnificent, large man, well groomed and all, got out and came strolling near to the lei venue where Fred Langley and June Nani were chatting.

Fred recognized him, he had met him before.

Fred commented, "Oh, good. Here comes that lawyer acquaintance friend of mine now."

Wallace ducked behind the lei venue.

"He's coming after me. I know it." Wallace asked for mercy, confessing, "I find towels and stuff on the beach a lot of times late in the evening. So I found this towel and some twenty dollar bills rolled up in it and it was late at the beach. I always check it out late in the day. It was two months ago. I knew it was abandoned. I thought."

Wallace walked from behind the lei venue. He stepped behind a bunch of leis piled high on display as the lawyer, who had gotten out of the car, was very cool. Wallace was watching from a corner as though he were shopping.

June Nani put up for Wallace as Mr. Thwarton was craning his neck to get a good look at him.

She said, "Oh, Mr. Thwarton. That is one of Fred Langley's buddies, Wallace. He likes it deep in the garden, he hikes in there with our other friends here. They're out there most of the time they come. One way or the other, with one or another partner, the hike on a trial is intriguing, refreshing, and interesting."

Wallace moved around and stood looking over rows of leis and flowers high on a shelf, corsages were wrapped.

Wallace explained, "I was out there on the beach one day and had to come back early after the sunset, the rain cloud blew in and quickly showered, some heavy drops. So instead of running, I picked up the towel and beach mat; and when I was going home I noticed there were dollar bills in the towel. I checked the towel and I thought the owners were accidentally, maybe, forgetting it."

June Nani was severe. She added, "Out with it. I saw you pocket two ti plant cuttings. What are you doing?"

Wallace stood up stiffly and handed June Nani a ti plant cutting from his pants pocket and five dollars in ones.

He said, "I'm taking this one, please."

June Nani lightened up.

She defended, "Sure Wallace."

Then, Mr. Thwarton was looking gravely at him and June Nani was considerate.

She said, "He'd just bought the one ti plant and had grabbed the two, the other by coincidence, he wasn't pocketing."

"Okay?" Wallace added.

Auntie June Nani said, "Alright, you can pay for the other one or give it back."

"Okay," Wallace said.

"Mr. Thwarton," June Nani proclaimed, "I'm not pressing charges."

Mr. Thwarton replied, "I'm not a cop, nor am I here for that beach towel or whatever else he found on the beach sometime. That's not my line of work."

Auntie June Nani asked, "Well, what are you here for."

He replied, "I'm just all excited about all the birds out there today. There are a lot around."

Wallace commented, "Ya, in the evening they really like to chirp away."

Wallace was relieved that there would be no pressure.

June Nani commented, "It's so nice around here. One thing you can count on here, evenings usually, the bird tree really lets loose."

Wallace commented, "Good, some birds are around. He was relieved everything was going so well; just so the bird tree was active in the evening and early afternoon, so Mr. Thwarton can feel relaxed.

Mr. Thwarton looked around and stepped back, winking at June Nani. They could tell he was in a happy time. An egret bird gilded around and perched on the nearby lawn, pecking out some morsel and tilting its head back, gulped it down. Mr. Thwarton was taken about on a flight of imagination mind addition appeasement. It was good that some mynah birds were prancing around.

Mr. Thwarton explained, "It's so nice up here in this uplands garden. It's a sight from that trail I know. I've been to the beach that way," he pointed, "and nearby.

"I've come to like listening to Sam and Frank when I'm up here. And if I'm doing a business deal for one of my clients just in town, I think I can find some fresh tropical fruits around here somewhere to take back. If I go that way," He subtly points to a noticeable trail on the other side of the parking lot to the side of the tall coconut trees, I think I can find some fruit around there somewhere. Up that way, there's a fresh artesian well; probably somewhere. Something growing somewhere by a nearby stream is wild, awapuhi (soap ginger). and thistle berries.``

And there were fruits there. Some ripe fruit of a native plant, soursop, seemed to beckon to be taken, it was looked at hungrily. Nearby was a ripe lilikoi (passion fruit), a wild vine, which was visible among the much foliage nearby a grove growing just beyond a fence.

Mr. Thwarted wandered to the lilikoi (passion fruit) area, the hedge nearby grew tall as a windbreak. He took several steps into the bush of the lilikoi vines leaning on the hedge and found one of the yellow, handsome fruits with both hands, gently twisting it round and round until it came off of the vine. Nearby there were some passion fruit flowers that would in time become the fruit.

Mr. Thwarton stepped back several steps and rubbed the fruit on his trousers, cleaning it, or like someone polishing an apple before consuming it, and smartly bit into the fruit.

Auntie June Nani was watching from across the sidewalk by the lei stand.

She described, "The lilikoi passion fruit blossom has a number of parts, the three in front are likened sometimes to a divinity. The colors, too, are notable."

Wallace commented, "They are really nice flowers; purple and white symmetry."

The ripe passion fruit Mr. Thwarton bit into was as he bit starting to ooze out its seedy pulp. He was careful as he was eating, spitting out the thick rind and holding the seedy pulp in his mouth. He swallowed it, its seeds included were all part of it. It relaxed him momentarily, the usual fruit juice staple was strong.

He smiled and looked at the numerous people gathering at the music site. And about twenty yards from him at the lei venue they were watching him. He smiled a little, he was happy to be there and enjoyed the fruit taste.

He rambled on, "I just like to hang out here where there's a bird flying, where all the birds are singing, where I might even find a ripe, ready-to-pluck coconut from one of the not-too-high coconuts."

There were some coconut trees on the other side of the hedge by the passion fruit. The Fiji Dwarf coconuts there were close to the ground, and when they bore, their big, beautiful fruit was easy to handle, one would bend over to twist off a coconut from its branch. Coconuts like these were treasured especially for their water, but they could also be counted on for providing a piece of pudding-like meat. These fruits were being grown commercially elsewhere.

Near this line of Fiji Dwarf coconuts was a line of coconut trees that grew above the height of a man, some were ten feet high, and they were all bearing fruit that could be considered to pick.

Mr. Thwarton liked coconuts. He looked at the coconut trees, these were from groves somewhere else on the island, and all of the trees could be picked from, their numerous groups of coconuts had passed the very young stage.

He looked up at one of the trees, and first, took off his shoes, and he wasn't one to wear socks, donned his aloha shirt for the occasion, he was wearing a neat designer tank shirt. He groped the tree's trunk and put his right foot high up the leaning trunk. his feet were now parallel to each other and if he moved one of his feet up a rung a little, the tree's trunk has subtle protrusions round about it, he could lean on it, keeping his hands about the trunk to insure he wouldn't fall the couple feet to the ground, and inch up to the groups of coconuts below the fronds. At this point, he used one hand to turn the coconut. If it was good, less than half a whole turnaround would set loose the coconut to the ground. He soon had a coconut to come down to; and carefully reversing the process of getting up there carefully returned to a few feet from where he could hop on down to the nice, green lawn.

He had twisted one around until it came twirling off and falling from the stem it was on next to about five or ten other coconuts. Having gotten a few such coconuts, which would have been removed by tree trimmers anyway, he had backed down several feet quickly before jumping a few feet to the tree base, he picked up a large, green coconut and walked over to Fred. He gave him one.

This was at the lei venue, and he asked Fred as he paused, if they would like one.

"Like coconut?" he asked.

"No thanks," Auntie June Nani and Fred said together.

He set the two in his car.

He added, "Thank you for telling me about this place, Fred."

Fred replied, "Ya, I heard about them a long time ago." He could have rambled on about his early days. "That's okay, Mr. Thwarton."

Mr. Thwarton rambled about for a while.

He mumbled, "Somewhere there is a fresh artesian well. Hardly anybody is somewhere out there. Near a stream, maybe the head of it."

As he rambled around for a quarter-hour, he arrived at one of the garden walk trails that quickly went into a gulch. He was soon on it and rapidly hiking away on it. This one had a running stream, a trail then that crossed it and ran along its side. This was where one could drink the water that was careening over the strewn round rocks. Some were little. Some were quite loose, there was a pool just downstream and the larger rocks formed a pool below a small waterfall.

Mr. Thwarton forgot about the artesian well he was looking for and enjoyed some of the drinking water from the running water into the pool. He cupped his right hand, dipped, and sipped. This relaxed him and he sat on a flat rock nearby and listened for the birds, which was unusual this time, because the stream echoed, and there wasn't but a distant mountain bird peeking through the foliage for a moment. But he watched the little waterfall for a while and headed back the way he had come, a fork in the trail he remembered took him back to the trail emptying into the park site. He viewed the lei venue site and rested.

After he got back to the lei venue site, he looked around at the coconut trees. There were several lines of very tall coconut trees on the opposite side of the parking lot, opposite to where the coconut trees he had climbed were. These old coconut tees were way up there. One dropped a coconut that landed with a thud.

This was a well-kept garden, and there were signs about these trees, 'Watch Out For Falling Coconuts'.

He wandered back to the lei venue, smiled at Marty, a new personage about there, and noted that Mr. and Mrs. Langley taking seats on some benches by the singers, Sam and Frank, and noticed Wallace was just leaving in his car. It was a while later.

Mr. Thwarton commented, "It's like I said, I just like to come up here and hang out. This is where sometimes the bird tree has a lot of birds singing. I might even like to find a coconut hat to buy."

Auntie June Nani looked surprised, perked up, and replied, "Mr. Thwarton, I have a couple of coconut hats woven by my nieces."

Mr. Thwarted replied, "I'll take one. How much?"

"Ten dollars."

He paid ten dollars for the one. June Nani took the money and let him have the crispy coconut frond woven hat, still quite green. But it would hold for a long time turning brown and fitting well.

Mr. Thwarton asked, "Is there some sugar cane?"

Auntie June Nani was proud of her native Hawaiian sugar cane stalks. They were about two feet long each,

each having about five segments. The end segment had a strip off the side that had broken off when it was hacked.

She replied, "That will be twelve dollars, my friend. You know this is Hawaiian sugar cane."

"I'll take two," he added.

Fred Langley thought that was interesting. For someone to come and buy anything but a lei. But then, he himself usually bought a corsage.

Marty, who had been around after roaming near a seashore trail jaunt, was relaxing in a row of park benches listening to the singers. He looked relieved to see his friends by the lei venue and noticed his friendly singers were there.

Marty came over to the lei venue and asked, "What's the law here for?"

June Nani replied, "He is a friend. All of my good customers are friends, Marty. Wallace likes him, too."

Wallace had just walked away toward the wide trail going past where the singers were lining up to do a special promotional set. He stopped by a mango tree on the other side of them as a ripe mango dropped nearby. He was walking by and took a step to where he could check it out. The lush lawn had padded the ripe fruit and it was hardly bruised at all.

Nearby were a few soursop trees in the bush, with loaded branches. There was a nearly perfect fruit.

And the mango he had was something he could toss and catch in his hand.

A moderate gust of trade wind picked up.

Wallace was lucky, he simply enjoyed mango fruit. This ripe fruit's peel had split just enough for him to pinch it and peel it back further. He bit into the beautiful, light orange-yellow pulp right down to the seed.

There was music starting up and it did not break its stride.

Wallace enjoyed peeling and eating the ripe mango, its juice dripped onto the grass below. He carefully bit into it down to the seed and scraped it just a little bit.

Good, he was carrying a handkerchief, and the mango refreshed him as he padded his face and hands.

The moderate slow breeze blew through the park, less gusting than other times. And everyone enjoyed it.

And the music was warming up. It could be heard at the lei venue, they had some small speakers. The benches were filling up with lei stand and lunch wagon customers when Mr. Thwarton was seen driving off. He lived on the other side of the island.

A host of tourists arrived in four limos.

Frank and Sam had warmed up and decided to sing "Flowers, Times". And Frank did an introduction to their singing, which was as Sam got into singing their standard.

Frank commented, "There was a time we went to the mainland to do promotional songs."

Sam paused and added, "This is somewhat what we performed there, "Waikiki Sand", which was recognized. And they did others,"Vacation to the Isles", "The Isles Holiday", "Tour Day Way", "The Hawaiian Islands", "Lookouts for You", "Go to the Islands", which drew a loud applause, "Oahu Room", also getting a standing ovation, "Tours and Beach", and a few others, i.e., "If You're Going To Hawaii", "Honey Darling Tour", and "Sweet Sunsets".

Mack could be seen walking by as he found a seat in time to listen to the rest of the show..

Frank and Sam, the little duo they were, hesitated first then put down their ukuleles after playing these songs for a few minutes more. Frank had a bag of pupus (snacks) and a thermos. Soon, after refreshing themselves with some of Frank's thermos cool iced tea, they were back to warm up for some more songs. After they had refreshed themselves,

Sam got up and displayed the recorded CDs of their work, which they had recorded when in a studio; these were quality recordings.

A new tour group was nearby as three of the cars of visitors filled up and left.The tour groups nearby wandered over the CDs and some people asked Sam and Frank about their musical efforts.

The first tour group person asked, "Is this, you guys?"

He was pointing to a CD with Sam and Frank close-ups on the cover.

'Yes, it is," replied Sam.

"Can I buy this CD?" asked the person.

"Why, certainly," replied Frank.

"How much is it?" the person asked.

"This one," replied Frank, "is ten dollars."

"I'll take two," the person said.

"One's a gift?" asked Frank.

"Yes," the person replied.

"Alright, that'll be twenty dollars," Frank said.

The person scooped up the two CDs and added, "Thank you."

"Mahalo," added Sam.

Mack came around and stood to the side. The tour guide and other CD buyers returned to their seats to listen to the others. June Nani's lei stand was busy and there were many from the tour group.

Fred Landley and Marty smiled genuinely happy smiles at the tour group who were enjoying listening to the songs. Fred and Marty were proud of Frank and Sam. And the songs went on.

Some of the visitors there were right pleased, they clapped and dropped money in Sam and Frank's upturned basket. The visitors had leis of plumeria recently purchased.

Actually, some bought leis from June Nani; many were customers.

Sam and Frank were ready to play. Sam was ready for a good question.

Frank asked, "What shall we play next?"

Sam replied, "We'll play our usual flower songs."

Another time, in weeks following, the scene was about the same. Frank and Sam had brought and tuned up their baritone ukuleles and introduced some songs.

As Sam and Frank managed to set their 'ukuleles down after an applause of visitors, so nearby sat Wallace, solitary staring up a hiking trail.

Wallace got up and started walking onto the hiking trail.

Frank, who was breaking, stood up and stretched his arms, Sam, too, was stretching his arms, and Frank leaned over.

Frank asked, "What shall we play now?"

Sam replied, "Well, let's play our usual flower songs and standards."

They were taking a full break, it was a long break, but it was soon over and time to do some of their songs, and they were debating on where to go in doing their repertoire.

"Aloha!" commented Frank. "We'll do a song with aloha."

Sam replied, "That must be one of the songs of the islands?"

"I guess so," Sam replied.

"We're doing the promotion run?"

"O.k., what song shall we sing, now?" asked Frank.

"Let's stay with the promotional few for now. The aloha song"

"I think it's okay." Frank offered.

"O.k.," Sam replied.

Soon their playing ensued, and at a moderately brisk pace. It sounded so good, they were definitely considering showcasing some instrumentals. The element of tourism was in the offering, it was a good choice to promote the island well. To show it this day was the "Tour Day Way" song, it was a good song and interesting.

Frank's solo playing the melody repeatedly slowly faded down as the signal they were about to sing. They hit it, which they did with a sudden start, which was with the second verse first.

As the song was over some of the attendees were leaving, and they had to catch their tour car rides. And both Sam and Frans knew what they had done was well done, and it was the applause that told them it was quite an okay song they delivered.

As the duo had CDs out front and to the side on a table for sale, and a few people were browsing them, not just the tourists who were just about to leave, but some of their local fans. Sam and Frank played on, they went first into the introduction of one of their light-hearted songs and noticed a lot of visitors were pausing at their CD table and going through their many various CDs out for sale.

As they were relying on their capos to give an alto ukulele sound from their baritone ukuleles, the accompaniment to their next song was with a long, repeating introduction, from which they paused and added, "A-lo-ha."

Their music went on with a loud point, and the pace was with everyone there, who was enjoying the music. It was another one of the songs that they did that was in their promotion set, it included a view of a tourist, and resident in a way that was appreciated by the visiting tourists and residents.

Some of the lunch wagon folks were nearby and hung out in front of their lunch wagon. They applauded with the visitors. Songs lingered in the air.

After the set and the performance, the performers were resting.

But they went on. The songs about the many visitors were changing.

There was applause after the song. A couple of people from the tour group took their picture and put several dollars into their upturned basket.

Another couple, who had been listening to their songs from the first introduction, got up and walked over to one of the nearby garden's adjacent trails.

There were birds flitting about. Some myna birds were on the green, green grass lawn near to the songsters as an upland bird, an 'o'u flitted about and smartly flew off again. There were pairs of small birds, and a flock of small birds hurriedly flying about.

Sam commented, "Wow! Did you see that little 'o'u bird?"

Frank replied, "Whew! Hey, yes I did."

Sam relaxed and gazed long and longingly when the small birds and the flock of small birds flew off into the tall trees surrounding one of the trails.

Sam added, "OK."

Frank commented, "A typical day then. This is when somebody is outback playing their music on their guitars."

Sam added, "That would fade out as a song could be heard. We're singing for about half of a minute, and that song fades out."

There was a pause as Frank and Sam were gathering their wits to continue singing. Frank was catching his breath to sing the intro. Most of the visitors who remained in the area were standing, ready to go to their waiting cars, but hanging on to every word Frank and Sam said.

"Mahalo," Sam said.

"Frank added, "That's thank you."

Sam and Frank picked up their instruments to the ready-play position but decided on a new tuning.

Sam asked, "The 'A' tuning?"

Frank replied, "Ya."

With a pause after this, they started strumming their introduction, and with the change of key the series of appropriate chords was with a differing fingering; they played a moderate beat, and the introduction most changed went right into the first verse. It was a slight change.

They were having a fun view of touring and tourism. While having gone on a tour once, Frank and Sam were going into the song, which was informative of the local color code, a custom of the Hawaiian Islands, and relating it to the particular islands at a time. It was with a good feeling and everybody nodded in agreement.

The small audience applauded.

"Mahalo," Sam said. "Thank you very much," he repeated.

Frank commented to him, "We could do this more often as a promotional statement?"

Sam replied, "That's a good idea."

Visitors from a tour group there were a few people who happened by. The small group of the audience also often included Wallace, Fred and Madeleine, and June Nani.

A small group from the tour group was taking pictures and walking about the place. They had just recently bought orchid leis and were wearing them.

Sam was asked to snap them. He was a friendly guy, he had an aptitude for taking pictures, and so he snapped away.

The tour group was getting comfortable, they got ready to listen to some singing by Frank and Sam. Some of them spread blankets on the lawn, some were on beach towels, and some were still sitting on the few benches that had been placed there by the lei stand people; a few of the group were happy to be standing up behind the benches as standing room attendance.

"I don't know?" chirped Sam, "What shall we play?"

Frank suggested, "Let's play "Lookouts for You"."

There was a little niche of the Frank and Sam Duo there, also, and they were like a garden of blooming marigolds, they were radiant. Sam played briskly with feeling at a moderate pace, and Frank joined in as the song they were into was in its introductory phase. They played "Lookouts For You", and then they paused.

This was sort of a break. First Frank stood up.

He informed, "I am Frank, and I've been with this little group we are, Frank and Sam, the Duo; and as a couple of years of the last ten years, we have been coming here and singing, usually, mostly, our own original songs."

Sam commented, "That's right. He's Frank, and I'm Sam. We have been playing our songs around for twenty to thirty years, some of the songs are from more than fifty years ago. Some of our tunes have changed a little in that time."

Frank added, "This song "Streams, Beaches, and Rain" may sound a little like, uh, "Breeze Melodies", I think it was part of it at one time."

"On with the show," called out a man on the bench in front.

"We're doing this next song," Frank informed, "it's kind of a grand music finale and we hope you like it. It's "Lookouts for You"."

"Thank you," the man who had called out said as he clapped. "On with the show, okay?"

Sam replied, "Okay, we're getting into it."

Sam and Frank played the intro and began to sing.

Frank and Sam were soon through with playing "Lookouts For You". This song had taken them a while to do with the instrumental passages, and the pause that ensued when they were through was so they could continue. Frank and Sam listened to the chatter that had been generated and looked about.

Frank commented, "This original song was once part of our repertoire. It has been greatly enjoyed, listened to, and as the distant mellow song it is. We play this often, and it may be heard on a CD. The CDs are for sale, so if you have a player, good."

This was a good sales word, which had faded with the bass track they had still going next to their microphones, it accompanied a light percussion but there was a bass booming in the distant, usually out of hearing, nether regions of the parking lot.

Sam and Frank waited until the air had stopped vibrating, which was a couple of m minutes, and until they had paused, they played their instrumental song, a new song and they continued telling the audience there about themselves. It was done over a quietly ascending percussion.

Someone was in a parked car at the far end of the large parking lot, and they had a boombox turned up. Their player was blaring a song about famous big wave surfing spots. Though it was faintly heard about the lei stand and park benches where Frank and Sam were strumming their ukuleles.

Wallace was between, and he paused and listened in this late, of the day, time as a few hikers were returning to their cars, starting them up, pulling out, and subsequently driving home.

Sam and Frank continued waiting and were satisfied it had quieted down. They played a few songs, and the verses of these were instrumentally treated as the intermittent vocals they sang continued on.

Sam listened for some applause. It came. It was light and sincere; then he looked, as Frank did, and applauded himself.

Frank commented, "This is going so good. Let's continue."

The visitors were so enraptured by everything they played. It was one of those very nice days that come every few weeks that is unbelievable in the idea of it just being another day, and it is a lovely day. In the evening after the group of patrons from the lei stand got comfortable in front of Frank and Sam, the duo went into their song with a long introduction. This was characteristic of their music. They played the song. It was early evening and there were still some tour group visitors listening; though some were leaving. Of those, some stopped and listened and looked around at the trees and flowers like they wouldn't be there again for a long time.

"What'll we play?" asked Sam. "Fern Forest" or "Fern Forest Blues"? "Maybe, "Downtown Uptown", or "Forest Birds"?"

Frank answered, "Let's do our good old "Oahu Room"."

"Okay," Sam replied.

Then Frank and Sam paused, as Frank addressed the dwindling audience.

He said, "In that this might be our last song of the day, which may surprise you is that some of you many visitors are with the local fans, be patient. We might do another song for an encore, just a second."

Frank and Sam played "Oahu Room" with its verve upward feeling, while some visitors who were standing remained listening as their cars were parked with the doors open. Wallace came over and took a seat where there had been several and Frank and Sam were now standing and belting out their song, this was a good song to stand and belt out. As soon as the introduction was over and they were singing, interrupted by several long vamp instrumental sections with changes of keys resounding with the original key as they started singing again, they had been spotlighting the various instruments they had at their disposal, Sam had picked up a harmonica and played the melody between verses, there were some applauding fans.

The audience applauded at the end of the song for a long time.

One tour group organizer was there, he was generous with the donations and many of his visitors followed suit by tossing in money, dollar bills accumulated to over seventy dollars in their coconut palm frond basket.

Fred and Madeleine Langley had been in the back of the visitor group, applauding the good, easy listening, music. They were enjoying the music and watching. Wallace, too, tossed in a five dollar bill as beheaded to the lei stand, which was folding its shutters.

The tour groups were parked about twenty-five yards away; a car was parked with more than six people from one, and a van carrying nine beside it was filling up the seats. These were tourists in their aloha shirt attire, which was not too formal for everyday wear, and their group had a lot of applause for them even as they were drifting away, turning around and applauding and listening to the last strains of a song. All of them would probably be enjoying their time in their hotel rooms later that night. The hotels might have lounges and groups playing.

Other groups of tourists, who had come to listen and were still there, were leaving. They were being taken care of by their respective hotel trams.

Another small group of visitors had been driven there by someone they knew, and they were looking for their host's parked car, which they found. There were three couples, the men and ladies of the group were going to a major hotel's dining facilities straight away; they would enjoy the dining and possibly retire without entertainment later that night as, perhaps, a few of the hotel roomers might drift to the lounge and enjoy the show by singers playing three sets.

Sam and Frank, even though it was late, were warmed up, and so were encouraged to do another one of their songs. One of their favorites came to mind, and after about a minute of wait time, they were introducing and playing, "Tours and Beach". But since most of their audience had left or was leaving, and they were getting tired from attending a couple of shows previously, they decided to finish up. As they packed up to go phone, Sam commented.

He said, "Come back tomorrow. We'll be here."

Sam and Frank left after the last visitors had left.

The next day a moderate wind blew across the azure sea below the lookout sites that had access from trails of the parking lot. This duo, who usually played their songs, was in front of the benches. The nearby lei venue opened as usual. Sam and Frank waved to June Nani, and she waved back.

Nonetheless, some unexpected visitors came to sit on the benches, others could be residents who were heading somewhere down a trail; to a seaside lookout, or up a gulch trail to a stream waterfall.

Some of the visitors who had been listening to them do their cover of "Aloha 'Oe" were returning this day to their homes. It was after the vacation and they looked forward to returns to their home states as well as eventual returns to the islands.

It was a nice day, a slow to moderate wind blew down the adjacent hills as, somewhat, a usual nice day.

Sam and Frank were soon warmed up to do some or another of their songs. This one was one of their favorites, this one was one they usually do. After about a minute of Frank and Sam playing and introducing themselves, their song "Tours and Beach" was repeated. It was the song that brought out some visitors' preferred practices. Getting suntanned was an option, go on a tour.

Many times visitors and tourists would go to spend time at the beach. When the group they were with had gone elsewhere on an all-day tour, they might just join them and enjoy a luau together that night. But on some days it was worth it to enjoy the beach. Watching the waves is comforting, and that was what many of them had come for. It was good to enjoy the good weather.

Sam and Frank smiled at the generous, small crowd.

Frank looked at Sam and smiled. They played the introduction of the entire song.

Frank commented, "This is unbelievably good weather."

Then, they went on introducing and playing into the next song.

There was a moderate breeze blowing as Frank and Sam, the duo, picked out an introductory refrain from one of the melodies of their song, "Streams, Beaches, Rain".

Sam started strumming hard his ukulele and Frank sat back for a moment and thought as if it was sort of a solo. After a moment, he too started strumming the rhythm for their next song. They continued with performing "Streams, Beaches, Rain", a song that resonated.

As they finished playing the song with duplicated choruses and singular vamps (a melodic bridge), the next song was getting a good build-up. A group of visitors sat on the benches.

Sam and Frank had gradually finished the song they were playing by repeating the verses, singing them twice; and playing the vamps (a certain musical bridge) each time it was taking on new dimensions as they did the verse or a new verse. They were a few minutes deciding on which song to do next.

It was a few moments of singing and the next song was getting a highly expected applause from the group of visitors, most were from a tour group, sitting on the concrete benches in front of their stage area, which was in front of an orchid display extending several feet above them.

Sam and Frank said, in unison, "Aloha".

"Aloha," Frank introduced. Speaking into a microphone was quite like singing into a microphone, but with the proper annunciation, he was also projecting the word out and up from his torso.

A moment went by and they looked at each other.

Sam said, "Try it again."

Frank replied, "Yes."

Frank and Sam (together): "Aloha."

There was a pause as they looked over the small crowd in front of them.

One of the visitors said, "Come back home with us and sing that song."

Up front on the first bench, a man held up his hand and was recognized by Frank sharply pointing a finger at him and smiling smartly. Sam looked at Frank in mock disbelief.

The man asked, "Would you come back to the mainland with us? I want to be there when you sing that song."

Frank asked, "You are in what part of the country?"

The man replied, "We're in the midwest."

 "We'll think about it," replied Sam.

Sam looked at Frank.

Sam asked, "We'll think about it!"

Frank looked out above the audience, he looked at the man and answered.

Frank replied: "Our trips to the mainland come and go. Maybe if you've got a travel location there, we can come and sing."

They were there to sing. And they sang the favorites of their homespun song. There was a moderate to brisk breeze blowing this afternoon as the duo introduced the refrain and introduction to the song they were so happy with.

Frank wanted to sing some country standards or some blues standards, but he was not that familiar with their midwestern song. Sam had some similar standards in mind to do. They liked to play a set, "When the Saints Come Marching In:, "Streets of Laredo", "Home on the Range", and "I've Been Working on the Railroad".

He asked, "Sam, do you know "On Top of Old Smokey?"

Frank replied, "I'm not sure."

They played their "Vacation To The Isles" song and the tour group people liked it from the start.

There was a minute of quiet as Sam played some of the set he'd mentioned on the harmonicas he had, he had a set and enjoyed playing the harmonica.

The minutes passed and Frank and Sam slowly got ready to play their next song, "Vacation Hawaii", which was really the opposite of going to the mainland.

Sam commented, "This song might go over well in a midwest town that was about a travel agency's setup."

Frank added, "A vacation in Hawai'i is liked even by the folks that live here; the luau is especially enjoyable."

Sam and Frank sang "Vacation Hawaii".

Mr. Thwarton had left his car, was happy to be in the area hiking around, and had come back. He was headed to the other side of the island, where he worked.

It was midday and for many was another busy week. Soon others came into the area, enjoying all the sights including a look at the lei stand, a look at the singer Sam and Frank, the aloha of the parking lot with its lunch wagons at one end, and trails on the other side of the coconut trees.

There were hikers often returning from around some corner of some trail that was just a pathway through the jungle.

June Nani the lei proprietor gave Frank and Sam for singing, some fresh cut coconut, from green coconut in a throwaway, paper, dish. The green coconut is the one that offers its elixir-like drink through a straw in the top, and straws in them are purchased regularly from a vendor nearby the lei stand, who was generous with sharing the coconut itself, a smooth, pudding-like refreshment.

A lot was going on and a moderate breeze blew through the area as the singers thanked June Nani who was like hosting them and returned to the lei stand while her nephew Max is selling lei after lei after lei to the tourists.

Sam and Frank went into playing their good old tune, Breeze Melodies. Sam introduced it as the first tone poem Frank had ever written, which was when he had been camping solo in a fern forest.

They also did "Flowers, Times".

Little Frank and Sam Duo were happy performing; they were happy with their performance, they were happy with the song they had chosen to sing and happy with the audience. So they bowed to the light applause of those who sat and listened. And there were among those who applauded, a tour group, and the tour guide also enjoyed and applauded the little performance.

Someone to the side was Mr. Thwarton, who had come again from his travels to the lei stand area. He actually was rarely on this side of the island, and yet he enjoyed the music, the time to forage for fruit, and enjoy the trails hiking a way or for a while.

Wallace, too, was around when he was hiking. When he was hiking, he laced up his ankle-length jungle boots and, rather than hike on a forest trail of which there were many close to the set, where Frank and Sam played their music, he was into hiking closer to the sea area. He had a friend, who had found a trail up to a higher lookout point and showed him the way on a previous hike. This time, there was so near to an abrupt, steep, straight-down drop of a hundred feet or so, even though into the tops of trees, that he was tempted to go some other way.

Wallace was engulfed in rainbows as he came out of the trail and headed up a switchback trail that led to a lookout.

As Sam and Frank were playing, not much was going on. And after a while of tuning their instruments, they too returned and joined the group listening to the songs by singing out one of their standards they usually did, "Pretty Red Hibiscus".

Sam and Frank were not too far from where Wallace and his hiker friend had gone this one day, which was into the bush so thick one had to usually, look, as it was, down to find the trail. They were out on the trail and still listening to Frank and Sam playing the lunch hour in the distance.

And since this was lunchtime, there was a regular lunch wagon near the trail opening at the parking lot. It was a sight for sore eyes to be welcomed for a lunch plate.

There they were, with some long lines, many tour drivers, and their patrons, who were often at these garden benches to buy leis and enjoy the singers. There were some who brought their own lunch among the tour drivers. And there were a few who tuned ukuleles and played in the parking lot quite a ways from where Frank and Sam were. The standards of which there were numerous had personal touches to their delivery.

Another time after the day had gotten late, most of the tours and tour drivers had gone home; then, lunch wagons were either being packed up and ready to go, or gone, and Frank and Sam came to play again their afternoon set.

This time, Marty and Fred Langley were just leaving for a mid-afternoon hike, which was usual for them. Hiking, it was from the place they usually went, to well on a trail that went toward a sea lookout. The songsters played as Marty and Fred were just heading to the trail entrance, which was across the parking lot, to the side of the main road, which curved upward through to a suburban ambiance park that also had benches.

Sam and Frank's fading faded out as Marty and Fred walked on. They were soon on their way to Fred's car, where they would head to a suburban street that had a cul de sac with a vacant lot and a small garden park. It was right next to a public right of way that did go well into a forest reserve. They were on the outskirts there.

Fred said, "This is but one trail that we may take if we want. Then, meanwhile, at the June Nani lei stand, she was talking to Mack, this one of her pineapple-picking relatives, who had come to visit her and was still looking for work in between jobs.

"Are you still looking for work in the pineapple fields?" June Nani asked.

Mack replied, Yes, June Nani. Almost every day I check for work."

June Nani replied, "Sometimes we need a little help here, you can come to middle-of-the-week packing leis, or stringing leis in the evening. I pay you good."

"Maybe I'll come, " he replied.

June Nani went on to face a tall customer who was buying a hundred dollars worth of leis, ti plant cuttings, and sugar cane cuttings.

Mack eyed him as he walked around the side of the little lei stand. After a while, he got on his bicycle and returned to his home in about fifteen minutes, smooth riding. He was away and perhaps looking for some white ginger plants.

Wallace, who had hiked out that day, had come again, and he was from his hike to visit there. He came from time to time to visit and talk to June Nani, and sit and listen to some of Sam and Frank's music. He found the long excursions of most days not so often. He went on to talk to June Nani, enlightening her on the state of the foliage, the fruitful path was well taken. On some hiking trails, he found some really nice places.

"Wallace commented, "I've hiked out and found some really nice hiking trails."

Wallace had often been hiking along a trailing edge near a lookout To him, it was relaxing to carefully hike along at a brisk pace, arrive at a lookout, hang gliders could be out, and perhaps as you watch the distant surf a hang glider could be seen gliding by; and then, you'd better hurry home before the sunset.

The audience, as usual, applauded at the end of the song.

While the audience, a mixture of tourists about straight off the plane, local friends, interested local fans of the music of the islands, and regulars of the lei stand and other businesses about the area of the parking lot, were attentive, they applauded after the song "Tours and Beach".

One of the tourists, a man, said, "Shouldn't I be on a tour of some important place on the next island and we could look it up?"

"I know what you mean," he replied.

Tours could take valuable vacation time so some visitors preferred to spend their time at a beach. Then, tours could take a break at an acceptable beach, or a roadside stand where they might buy sea shells and other times, or a mountain seaside lookout.

The tour that was taking their time sitting in on Sam and Frank's ramble and song fest were those on vacation. Their time was somewhat like visitors, the preferred way was to spend some time at a beach, then when it got really hot, they could head to this hiking trail, or coconut and lei stand they had heard about.

The tours would come, and the visitors might buy sea shells if there were some from another stand or at the lei stand. Other items were interesting, one was a gourd helmet with feathers on top.

"I'd like a feathered gourd for my nephew," said the man.

June Nani replied, "These are for warriors, my man."

"That's o.k., we'll set it in a window sill and dust it from time to time," he replied,

June Nani lectures Wallace, Fred and Madeleine and her other patrons, "For years people have been coming to experience the islands for themselves. They have heard about it, and now they come. Many come on tours to the islands, to tour and experience what they have always heard and dreamt of. For the most part, the islands are a paradise. To come here is the maximum benefit. Paradise is heavenly."

Little did the man know, the gourd with see-out places and feathers, was a helmet placed on a young man once, for life.

June Nani lectured Wallace, Fred, and Madeleine, among her other temporary patrons such as tourists in the back. She lectured, "For years, people who have been coming here ask how to experience the island for themselves?" They had heard that it would be neat.

"And now then come. Many come to tour from here to the other side of the island, they go to the other side and stay overnight at a peaceful cove; return the next day, and tour on to the other major islands, the outer islands.

"And what they experience is an, 'I have always heard about Hawaiian sunset'. Some of them had dreamt of coming for more than a year. They've saved their hard-earned money to come to the island. For the most part, most of them see the islands as they are, a paradise, their moments here are blessings for them, and they return to remember and perhaps come to attain. To come here on this island, there can be some maximum benefits. One man comes here to pick his favorite coconut, he also likes it because paradise is heavenly and there are blessings in heaven."

"I hope so," replied Mrs. Langley.

Madeleine Langley was happy to be visiting the lei stand again, her husband was around somewhere.

She commented, "I hope there are blessings."

June Nani added, "Oh! Yes, it is really possible to have the blessing just by being here on the island, though some places pervade a higher blessing. That is why so many of the people that live here come, park their cars, and go hiking up a trail; many are the blessings."

Mack was around and visiting June Nani. He asked Frank and Sam if they could play one song he liked, "Downtown Honolulu". They agreed.

Mack had been hanging around when visiting June Nani's. He strolled to where Frank and Sam were set up and playing. There were a lot of empty benches, and the tour drivers were gone. The tourists were gone with them, and there were some local friends of Frank and Sam's as well as regulars such as Mack from the lei stand.

Mack asked, "Frank and Sam, could you play one song?"

Frank replied, "If you liked the show we just did, which was a long one, you might like this song "Downtown Honolulu".

Sam added, "You often go by Honolulu, downtown?"

Mack replied, "Yes, I do."

Frank said, "O.k., we will do it."

Sam proceeded to adjust the mic stands, turned on the bass accompaniment they had recorded, set it to the song they were going to do, and bowed his head in a moment of rest in anticipation of some wild instrumental bridge accompaniment and ending.

Some time went by and then Frank and Sam sang "Downtown Uptown". They were just finishing presenting their newly developed set. Their songs would roll on one after another for a few songs, like a concert. It was sort of a mini-concert of mostly their promotional songs, which went on for a few hours including standards before they ended with a new original tune. It was good listening to them sing. And the visitors enjoyed "Downtown Uptown".

There was some time before Frank and Sam sang "Downtown Uptown". They had just finished presenting their newly developed set and had had a sandwich.

The new set rolled on, it would be memorable, and one after another of the friends and patrons from about the lei stand strolled by. A few songs were played, and the mini concert of promotional songs was their practice since it would be like a concert where they went. The hour included the standard "Pretty Red Hibiscus" once more, and before it ended was with a newer promotional song, "Honey Darling's Tour".

The little audience was enjoying their recurring "Downtown Uptown" song, the one that somewhat portrayed the singleton life.

Mack commented, "It was good listening to the song, a visitor may enjoy downtown, too."

They were ready to do another set.

Some of the local people at the site were returning to their abodes.

The friends and proprietors of the site were returning. Some went to their homes, some were hotel guests, some of the tour drivers ate a plate lunch then headed to their company's parking lot, and some were from there, they would return to their apartment or house.

"Bye, bye, you all," said the driver of one van, its passengers previously returned from an all-day tour.

June Nani went on, "These flower garlands are reminders for somebody who likes it here to return. Rather than staying at home, they come here. We're here and we are around to welcome them."

Wallace commented, "Some would just as soon stay at home."

June Nani continued, "Here, or on the beach, friends, and relatives are enjoying themselves just like when they go where there are a lot of shows."

June Nani was there, she and Mack stood together from halfway between where the lei stand and the singers were.

June Nani commented, "The flower leis are for somebody who likes to return, they are reminders of being here in the isles, and an open invitation to someday return."

Mack added, "Some of them will come back."

June Nani said, "If they like it here, some would rather come here than stay at home; and they will come here. We're here, and we'll see they are welcomed when we see our lei on them."

Mack added, "I hope so."

June Nani added, "I know."

Wallace, who was often around at this afternoon time, was returning and resting from a hike by the seaside trail. He stood near June Nani and Mack.

Wallace commented, "There are some off-road tours. I went down a gulch and there was a hiking group from a beach road parking lot trail."

June Nani added, "From here, the beach is a long trail, and finally they have a beach parking lot. I know some of our relatives will enjoy it."

Wallace added, "They like it when there are a lot of shows."

June Nani said, "They have beach shows. Maybe Frank and Sam go there sometimes and play their songs."

Not too far away and sometimes the Langleys and others are around listening to the singers, Frank and Sam.

They often meet at a park up the road from the lei venue, which has a large parking lot so near the mountains.

Nearby where June Nani and Wallace were talking the Langleys came and parked. They came to listen to where Frank and Sam were. And Frank and Sam were waiting for a few minutes for the audience benches to fill up; this afternoon was a really nice one.

The Langleys had parked a way down the parking lot and quietly, and calmly sauntered up to where their friends June Nani and Wallace were standing between the singing area and the lei stand. Some of the food trucks had packed and gone home.

The mountains were not so in the distance, a trail or two could be taken to further explore the forest and streams.

A thunderstorm could border on the empty sky and linger there at times, perhaps as the thunderstorm goes northward, fringing on the mountain tops and empty sky's edges. Some flashes of lightning occur usually more toward the mountains.

In the distance of the mountainous trails from the parking lot northward could be seen thunderclouds, though there were some flashes of lightning, thunder was so far away in the central part of the island, the storm clouds remained fringing off the mountains and gulches in the distance allowing the empty pale blue sky's background to be markedly profound edgewise.

Wallace looked at the meteorological phenomenon and thought, I will tell Anita when I get home, the storms are passing by northward. June Nani and Mack, both took a sigh of relief as it appeared the thunderstorms were indeed well in the distance and appearing to stay there; going to dissipate and drift seaward producing also perfect winds for the surfers on the waves out there. The Landleys were confident in good weather, it had been nice for them, it seemed, for a really long while.

Wallace had been in the mountains and looked often from a high pass to the distant seashores.

Scents of floral essence surrounded June Nani's lei venue, which had once been a small residential cabin. At her residence, which was several blocks from the parking lot, several blocks further and near some gardens, there are usually stores of flowers offering their odors of wonder. She worked some out of her home.

The regulars of the lei venue family had often visited this lei stand, stopping sometimes at the place where many leis were strung. Wallace visited too. The garden where Madeleine strolls is quite lovely, a bamboo grove holds its own with but some sparse grasses about its base by the side of those kukui nut trees.

Then, sometimes, there is a duo playing ukulele and singing nearby. Madeleine browses by there, sits on a park bench, and listens.

Wallace hiked sometimes to a favorite lookout.

Wallace, who had been in the mountains this day, had often looked across the tops of trees and houses from a barren passageway around a slight bend, pausing at the apex of the trail's bend. The distant seashore was stretching both ways, somewhat perpendicular about a mile away. Wallace had hiked to a lookout; a favorite because it overlooked a valley and seashore.

Above him and to the side north, mountain walls too steep and foreboding were the sites hardly hosted anyone, they were so steep, restless, and trailless. If he had brought his wife, Anita, she would have just stayed, where he was, where he was staying, on the trail where hardly anyone passed; to the side in a small tent.

The rustic trail he had taken started at the parking lot of the lei venue's south end about a half mile from where the lei venue was situated. Wallace had hiked to a favorite, familiar trail, it had a lookout toward the beach and a dry round rock stream bed interspersed with jungle foliage; if it rained a lot it might gush.

The lei venue was somewhat busy, sometimes the singing nearby by the Sam and Frank Duo could be heard. Nearby these areas, Madeleine Langley was resting comfortably while her husband, Fred shopped for a corsage for her. The gardens nearby where she had been, had also been visited by Wallace the day before. About the bamboo grove there were kukui nut trees, their nuts usually on the ground beneath their trees were just browned, on the trees the nuts were brown-green. About the bamboo groves were California grass, and elephant grass on the other side, both yards of these grasses were about waist high of the grass. A barren trail traversed through the shallow bamboo groves. Madeleine had been looking for bird nests.

The regulars of the lei venue were family. June Nani kept an eye on Wallace, he had a notion to have some unusual cuttings. The Langleys were about and browsing.

It usually smelled tropical floral, good around the lei stand. When the wind was brisk which was fairly usual, the flower smell, which was mostly plumeria, was thinner; though gardenia could catch on the breeze and perk one's senses up.

Wallace, an island person, likes to get off the island from time to time, typically going to the mainland to visit friends or relatives. The desert there has reminded him of perpetual island landscapes, and he has friends nearby on the mainland, who offer him a perspective change. On a visit, off-road to the side of many roads, a roadside park stretched long distances. He returns to his home and visits the lei venue.

He went to the mainland for two months between summer and spring three years before. He noticed the rainy season had possibly gone a little into the dry season this one year. Another year he didn't notice.

And Wallace is usually staying on in the islands.

In pre-discovery times picking up seashells, anything, from a beach was possibly frowned upon if not actually forbidden.

And Wallace was one to go to the beach regularly looking for things there.

An evening's cloudiness has a particular character to it. It's far from sparse cloudiness but there is a cloud. This is another day, a good day for Wallace as he goes to the beach.

Wallace visits deep valleys to find a difficult view of the sea and often visits the lei venue before mid-morning.

This one time he looked over a few orchid leis, mixed (orchid and plumeria, carnation and orchid, carnation, orchid, and pikake) and others and corsages that were on display. As he returned a few of the plumeria and gardenia blooms to their holders, they had been sitting in a vase with water in it, he looked to the part-owner and person looking after the leis and selling them, his long-standing friend, June Nani.

Wallace still found time to find his way through a dense foliage trail to a waterfall.

Some airline passengers en route to the islands were happy to look out the window at the distant pastel sky and thunderclouds as they approached the islands. These travelers were getting about the same views as many of the people on the island were looking northward. And not long after their landing, checking into their hotels and resting up, dining and further resting up before they take in a show or a performance at a club or on a big stage, they come to the June Nani lei stand and buy flowers and leis before they go somewhere else. This is where wearing a lei is normal.

Those members of the June Nani family, some *were* adopted, who are into the narrative *of* legends of the times, are most often selling car insurance. Some of the family members were moonlighting as cab drivers; there were considerable cab companies with them.

Usually, the narrative session goes on for an hour or two. The meal, which is with a variable pattern of comings and goings, there was as most large families may have, the narrative session. And this was at June Nani's residence, which has a large living room and dining room. The narrative session (*goes*) on for up to an hour or two before a meal. The main meal of the day is usually with these goings-on, quite sumptuous.

There was a traditional thing going on, a talk story going into oral history. like someone interviewing someone, this was traditional. Of the islanders with oral histories backgrounds, which might be where the regular event of the regular speaker starting out, declaring the recent weather, and the neighborhood's family and associates, many adopted persons, was in the recent times.

This oral history was a starting point. In the sessions, the speaker sets to declare personal events, of the likes of the members of the family, and if it was who was sick and why, there were points of sympathy. Then, the oral history session might and often did go where it could, into who was giving birth, who was recently born, and who was getting married. And how the children and the other family members were doing in the community could, would, and did go on dovetailing to the past generations in a traditional set that could go back to historical events of previous generations.

When the talk got inventive, and indeed the subject of food came up, the supporting oral tradition rhetoric was a really intense statement, one that couldn't be more accurate and respected. It could be found on an individual level. These were respected tales, usually, and some statements of some such historical events that preceded current generations could take the form of long orations with detailed accounts. Chant and hula are rather a part of some such deliveries in some cases.

So older family people giving attention at mealtimes filled in for the regular June Nani talk. The respected tales of the oral tradition usually found their way into numerous songs by songwriters and singers. Some statements of some historical events and people were loosely adopted there.

June Nani, the elder lei seller often sang a song. She hummed the tune the songwriter singers sang, "Grandeur of Flowers". She sang softly sometimes when working; it was a really good thing for her. Keeping accounts of the lei venue business also could be fun. And giving it a little more feeling, she sang. The work of keeping the leis and selling them that took precedence; she listened to the singers in the near distance, was rewarding..

Wallace, who had found his way to numerous high spots for overlooking the distant seas on many occasions could describe an event, if there were anything noteworthy, to his friends at the lei venue. June Nani had a lot of patience.

While June Nani had sung and hummed for a while, she was confident it was the songs the singer-songwriters sang.

Wallace, back from a two-hour hike on a trail, one hour to a lookout, where there were guava trees and he could pick a ripe one to refresh himself, and back. June Nani, noticing he was back and looking over the for sale collection, handed him a usual small bag of fresh hibiscus buds, a delivery made to her was usually early in the day.

"Thank you," Wallace thanked. "I appreciate your taking the time to gather the buds for me, you know I like these, and they are not usual for sale items. Thank you."

Wallace, who had been to a take-out restaurant four hours earlier had left a thermos with hot tea, the lid had kept the heat on it, so he quickly put the hibiscus buds in with the hot tea, and put the thermos top back on. Several moments later he talked to June. He drank a little of the tea, which served to erase a slight eeriness he had acquired this day on his hike, walking carefully to walk the trail would do that, he thanked June Nani. He paid the saleslady.

Some of the hibiscus buds that she had for sale came from a lush hibiscus hedge to the side of her front hard, June Nani had gathered the buds from the hedge before coming to the lei stand.

She looked at Wallace, who was sipping his tea.

She asked, "Is everything alright?"

Wallace replied, ``Yes, these buds are just fine."

Wallace was checking the flowers on her for-sale flowers at the lei stand. Gardenia flowers sat in small vases. Their thickness, their aroma strength, and general character were a texture of thought.

June Nani checked him out, she looked at him enjoying the hibiscus bud tea. And with approval, she was hoping he would buy some more of the leis and flowers, though there was no lack of customers and she sold out every day.

If Wallace had been as he did, roaming a dense valley trail, perhaps to go up by the waterfall site, it was not unusual. Alongside the trail around the top of the waterfall, one could get a nice, distant view of the sea, and very narrowly the seashore, where waves sometimes broke, their white lines rolling up the beach and disappearing one after the other being noticeable.

He was back at the lei venue, and he looked around for his friends. The Langleys were friends with Wallace, especially Fred Langley, who also enjoyed the music and outings about the lei venue.

One of Wallace's other friends, who was acquainted with the Langleys, Fred and Madeleine; there was Marty, a man from a sailboat visiting the islands from the West Coast. Wallace had met him there the week before, and now Marty was acquainted with the Langleys. He was often somewhere about a forest trail, walking to or from fruit areas, resting on a park bench about the songwriters, or just nearby the park entrance to the gardens, which was where once, he was within a loud, vigorous, vocal call. If one really tried, and Wallace had, they could call there.

Many were the wonderful blooms Wallace and many visitors, often tourists came and bought out the corsages and leis. It was a part of their daily life for June Nani, to sell out. The enjoyment, the enhancement of delightful scents, was a source of commitment, contentment, pleasure, joy, and purity, which they enjoyed. They were like most islanders, they liked everything, and partook of the goodness of the land. And the sales lady, June Nani, sang softly on her own.

The song June Nani sang was one she acquired from repetitive listening to the melody and numerous verses that had been in the air from the singer-songwriters. The words had worked to evoke a passion in which the joy she felt was given by the singers, and the listeners enjoyed being quiet and listening. Wallace, too, who felt it was in the manner of a visitor to so enjoy the songs, comfortably seated as the flowers were pausing, listened and slightly teared up thinking of the joy of the flowers that lingered even after they left the site.

The songs she patiently listened to were songs wove with varying loudness and a varying tempo that was as natural as someone talking the language. Indeed, the singers were receding verses and singing songs included in a natural talent they had. She was a good listener who listened to the vocalists over time. Sometimes they sang on a stage.

Wallace was there. He stood by June Nani listening to and appreciating all of it. As the lei vendor started selling leis, she went on as the songs were through the bushes and trees. It was a nice day, and there were plenty of customers who sometimes bought vases and flowers.

The songs of the songwriters were long verses, often repeating, and they could come and go as they were the singers. The verses they sang would be in the next song, its purpose being, perhaps, appreciation of the many flowers and local scenes. The scents were in the air. The lei vendor listened on.

The grandeur of the flowers was, perhaps, getting a more pompous outpouring from somewhere within themselves.

As Wallace was hiking the deep valley trail, he found the crossing to a stream.

About the lei stand, there were patrons.

The song rang true.

She paused in her singing, catching her breath, looking aside as Wallace applauded also. As Marty came about there smiling, if the Langleys had been there they would have asked June Nani to sing another song, if there was time.

And then she proceeded to hum the song "Flowers in the Wind". Marty liked that, and he handed her the ukulele from under the counter of her lei stand. Then, as she was pausing, and quickly tuning its 'A' string, she plucked out the melody and then continued she was easily accompanying herself in singing "Flowers in the Wind".

Wallace's chosen trail, which crossed a rocky stream with cool drinking water, was followed, also by groups of visitors passing the other way.

June Nani paused and looked at some of the people talking who were from a tour. They were coming near where she was.

"And does the song "Flowers in the Wind" go on?" asked Marty.

"Yes, it does," June Nani replied.

And then she went on easily enjoying playing the song she sang, which she had had in mind for most of that morning.

In the afternoon things were regular. In the distance of a near suburban town area, the friends of the lei stand and June Nani were hiking around and exploring along well-trod pathways. Fred Langley and Wallace Nottingham were about and enjoying the walk. They were through with lunch, having a delicious plate lunch gave them something to walk off. As a diminishing breeze that day yet flowed through the pathways they walked, on the sides of the paths were hedges of the hibiscus flowers, these were red hibiscus, and nearby were white hibiscus and orange hibiscus. They dipped and bounced in the breeze. Nearby shade trees were year-round.

"These hibiscus flowers have wide petals," commented Fred Langley.

Marty replied, "Quite like the flowers on the large trees over there?" replied Marty.

"I guess so," Fred replied.

The nearby road had a few very large, old trees to the side and the trees dropped some needle-like clump blossoms.

"These trees," Wallace added, "are from Central America.:

Fred added, "They are immense."

"Considerably," added Fred.

How many there were was hard to say.

Fred asked, "How many of them are there here?"

Fred replied, "About four."

There are these large trees along the corners of the road?"

"Yes."

Meanwhile, back at the lei stand, June Nani could be heard singing. As the songsters nearby the lei stand were taking a break there was a good quietude for her to sing on.

The day, like many, was nearly clear skies. Nearby the parking lot shade from coconut trees was shadowing the curb. In the distance, Sam and Frank, the young performers were tuning up their ukuleles for a little showtime. They had their songs ready.

At the mic, "Aloha," exclaimed Frank, "we hope you enjoy the music, this song is a good one."

As they started playing the song a moderate trade breeze, as usual, came briskly up and slowly passed. The winds went through the ambiance of the park, lei stand, flower gardens, performers area, nearby flower gardens (heliconia), and on down to the somewhat distant ocean there.

As the performers were performing, nonetheless, another group of the touring songs was being listened to by visitors, who had come up and quietly sat on the back benches. These visitors were hosting locals, hosting visitors friends of theirs, and they complemented the music with their humility and slight bowing to the quietly repetitive instrumental parts of the good songs Sam and Frank played. Some of these people snacked on some goodies they had brought with them, one or two had a thermos with their own hot drink, and packaged pastry items with that kept them well satisfied.

Not far away, June Nani was tending to the lei venue location she had come to for so many years. She was near enough to get a glimpse of the performers, and she listened to them from nearby, a two-row, small group of average coconut trees laden with fruit.

She was at the lei vending site and walked back to right in front to enjoy talking with a few customers, friends of hers who had come with visitors that were there in separate vehicles. There was a duo, Sam and Frank, that they listened to; the ongoing music nearby. The duo Frank and Sam continued to perform. There were young people with their parents there, young teens, and the singing went to their song, "Birds, Waves".

Wallace had come and paused as he was looking for a place to hike. He was always going to hike, he passed over the entrance trails on the other side of the parking lot beyond the coconut trees close to the road, squatted and rummaged in his hand surplus backpack for something of his day's store of meals, the food and water were light and nourishing. He found a trail that he had been on before and started on it, and out of sight going past a small grove of plumeria trees blooming as usual.

The newer newcomer Marty had come and paired up with Fred Langley as they were about to listen to the singing in the near distance. They had plans.

Fred asked, "Let's visit the urban area parks."

Marty replied, "OK, that's out past the twelve haole lehua trees?"

Fred added, "Yes. I'll drive. It'll take only less than ten minutes."

The immense trees overhung the road as Fred drove on.

Wallace, who had gone for a hike had come back nearby where, on a fence there a sign was on a gate to the large yard there, it read, World's Largest Heliconia Collection.

Just below the nice sign was an older, cockeyed sign a little weathered, it read "kapu" (keep out).

Wallace was back and around the lei stand. He stood nearby listening in awe to the rapturous singing of "Flowers In Wind" and "Birds, Waves". The songs like "Pretty Red Hibiscus" were also in their repertoire and came to the forefront momentarily.

Wallace had once been invited by someone from behind the gate who happened to be there. On his visit, Wallace asked, "Is this your heliconia collection?"

'No, it's state-owned," the caretaker replied. "I just work here."

Wallace explained, "I was once invited to come and look around at the labeled plants. Do you caretaker here?"

The caretaker replied, "I have friends come here and picnic. And they did come here more than once even taking pictures."

Wallace admitted, "I heard my friend Fred Langley comes here, goes inside, and looks around sometimes."

The caretaker replied, "That might be him I've seen here."

On the way to where the singer-songwriters were playing their songs, and others were there, a host of mountain apple trees had been dropping their purple blossoms. He was late for an appointment and hurried to his car and drove off.

In the distance the song being sung was plain, informative, entertaining, and somewhat beautiful, "Flowers In Wind" rang out like a shrill bird call, yet sung softly.

June Nani was patient and kept tending in her day to the many corsages she had for sale. One visitor from a tourist car was satisfying her want for customers and buying lots of leis

June Nani asked, "Is that your car over there?"

The visitor replied, "I guess so. I came to look over the corsages. Do you have orchids?"

June Nani answered, "Yes, there are a few left today." "OK, I'll take two."

After a while, little June Nani sang her song. She sang "Flowers", one of Frank and Sam's songs. She progressed in her singing, and the visitor sighed.

"Thank you," the visitor commented.

Marty and Fred, who had gone exploring in Fred's car, returned. They were just returning to the lei venue where there were so many well-placed coconut trees, haole lehua trees, papaya gardens, and orchids by a park bench. Not only were they finding Wallace there, comfortably listening to the little duo sing, but June Nani had joined him in the back row while she let her newest nephew tend the lei stand. June Nani was asked to do some singing.

Frank asked, "Come on, June Nani, come up here and sing with us?"

"Oh, no," she replied. "I've got to go back to the lei venue real soon. My nephew Mack is tending to it, and he isn't familiar with everything there."

Wallace, who had come while she was singing, had hung out and gotten comfortable in the side benches. Nonetheless, Wallace came to the lei stand and started browsing.

Mack asked, "Anything you want, Wallace."

Wallace asked, "I found some interesting ti plants recently. I wanted to know if there were some bunches of fresh ti leaves. I'd like some of them, too."

Mack replied, "There were some bunches of fresh ti leaves here. Just a minute." He started moving things around to see if there were fresh ti leaf bunches.

Marty and Fed kept their distance and were just able to hear June Nani's singing. It was sweet, some of it was the same song as the singer-songwriters sang. The time passed with this singing quickly.

It wasn't long before Wallace appeared. He strolled to the front of the lei venue, which caught the attention of June Nani; she stopped humming as it was at that point. Marty, who had left Fred to listen to the singer-songwriters came and was soon perusing the valuable merchandise June Nani had for sale up front and on top.

Marty asked, "Where can I buy some of those ti plants?"

June Nani replied, "Most days I have them, some are stated and well sprouted out. But if you want to be sure of getting a fresh ti plant, come early, okay? There are fresh ti cuttings but they sell out pretty early."

Marty added, "Okay, not today. But I'll come early sometime, maybe next week."

Marty continued looking at the various curios and floral presentations. He wandered around from the front to the side, he noted there were a couple of ukuleles for sale and coconut frond hats among the hat bands and shell leis. He paused and looked around nearby. He viewed the distant Dwarf Fiji Coconut trees, these coconut trees were in a row of four a ways from the parking lot between the lei stand there and another row of tall coconut trees. Some had maturing coconuts on them, and some of the coconuts were ripe, matured, and turning brown. And still further away across the parking lot were some tall heavily laden coconut trees. This part of the parking lot was really old, there were rises in the asphalt there from nearby tree roots pressing up on it. On one curb was green moss on the east and south side of the curb, and mosses were on the breaks rising on the parking lot asphalt surface. These mosses were very slow-growing, like the tall coconut trees.

June Nani was watching Marty, and Wallace was also watching him like a hawk, he was very protective of June Nani and the lei stand. Marty was a newcomer and seemed suspicious to him. Nonetheless, Wallace came and took a couple of leis. He returned one and carried the one for his purchase.

Wallace said, "I'll take two plumeria leis, one orchid lei, and a small orchid corsage for my friend, Madeliene Langley. I'm sure she would like one."

"That's okay with me," commented Fred Langley, Madeleine's husband, who kept a watchful eye on her. He was gruff and hearing Wallace was buying her a corsage made him somewhat overbearing, Fred was known for his jealousy.

June Nani declared, "Okay, Wallace. That'll be sixty-five dollars. If you want ti plant cuttings they'll be in tomorrow morning, I think my nephew Mack will be bringing them, and they are five dollars each."

Wallace added, "Okay. Just so they're not being mailed to me." Wallace left the lei stand area, walked to his car, got in, and drove home to his home. His wife Anita had said to come home early.

In the meantime, June Nani was singing along with the song the singer-songwriters were singing. Some new customers came from the tourist sector, she smiled at them and they, too, listened to the singing. And to the myna birds, who were playing around on the pavement opposite the large coconut trees.

It was not too far to the nearby garden bench where sat the gentleman songwriter singers. Frank and Sam were not in their usual place in front of the orchid wall, the orchid wall was made of orchid plants and was part of the garden's outlay. They were on some benches in front of other benches. They were not backed up by the orchids arranged like a shell. Such orchid arrangements were not unheard of and they were lucky this park area had some. They were just a couple of singer-songwriters, musicians seated on one of a group of benches watched them, some of them kept time to the melodies that were in the air. Both Frank and Sam, who were OK musicians, kept some songs swooning in the air.

For a few moments, while the singer-songwriters were first tuning their ukuleles, the strings stretched to a perfect pitch, and there were some nearby strange sounds. They ignored the strange sounds. In tuning, Frank hummed, Sam tuned from one string, and they warmed up on simple songs of their own. They paused and the audience found contentment.

Frank commented, "It's a nice botanical garden nearby."

Sam added, "Yes, these gardens are a pleasant experience. I like the green lawns."

Frank commented, "It is so nice the plants are great for holidays."

Sam added, "The island lei stands are great for that."

"Maybe we can go to a seaside park and look out to the sea.:'

"I've got a room with a view."

"It's nice to overlook the surf, we can go out there with our imagination."

Frank added, "Bless your room with flower blossoms, get leis, get corsages, get flowers in vases,"

As a couple of limousine tours were stopping by the lei stand, they were also stopping at a beachside shell stand, where sea shells were being sold. And they usually did well, with tourists, and sometimes locals, buying a cowry, or a conch shell. Everyone liked to try and play a conch shell.

The salesman there shows, "It's like a trumpet, you buzz your lips." He played a long, resounding tone.

Tours were stopping to listen.

Sam and Frank took this as a time to play one of their songs. Frank recognized it as the song they often played. Soon, the distant conch shell was fading out as that music, which was then an accompaniment, continued.

"Waves Rainbows," was one of the long-introduction songs and was faintly heard nearby. Nearby, Madeleine Langley, who had been hiking, came out of the dense foliage trail.

She paused and caught her breath, after hiking on the trail for a little less than a mile, which was posted, she sat and rested where she liked. There she could, and did hear the calm songs of Frank and Sam. She was, however, aloof from others, including friends of the lei stand, and the relatives of the person selling the leis. She spent a long time residing on one of the benches there and a coconut tree nearby gave her some shade.

Frank and Sam noticed she was listening, and they played "Waves, Rainbows" a second time as it was being listened to and enjoyed. They played moderate music of their own songs, the music was soft. And not forcing a breeze.

The lei venue did good business as Frank and Sam played their flower songs, "Flowers" first. This song was now in place of "Waves, Rainbows".

June Nani, the lei vendor, strung some of a lei, hanging long strands for customers to pick one out as usual, they would be tied as a lei bought. As the song "Waves, Rainbows" was a long song and faintly heard, attendees got comfortable. The song had a resounding repetitive ending.

The small crowd sat there for a moment, the audience reveling in the song had smiling faces. Appreciation was for the song they just heard. Sam glanced at the familiar faces, visiting people sitting quietly listening and quietly applauding after each song and a few familiar fans. The song was over, it was time for a little break.

He slowly set his instrument down, Frank did the same, and there was a momentary pause, as they bowed humbly and continued a long saying of thank yous.

Before too long, they were picking up their instruments to play their songs again.

In the meantime after this, Fred Langley and Marty Chadwick, who had journeyed away in the Langley car, and had found a nice suburban park and garden with dining facilities, came back. Their drive of about five miles away was leaving them back and parking, sitting and chatting and having a good time; all within the sound of the singers.

They had walked through one of the vast gardens there. About halfway through their walk, there was consideration for lunch.

Fred asked, "Why don't we have those mahi-mahi dinners from one of those diners?" He pointed to a couple of lunch wagons in a nearby parking lot that had tables; and take-out.

Marty replied, "O.K. You going to get something for Madeleine?"

Fred added, "Yes, just before we head back to the lei stand."

Fred and Marty enjoyed their plate lunches, Fred had a beef stew and rice and Marty had a mahi-mahi sandwich. And Fred was buying; a mahi-mahi plate (takeout) to take back to Madeleine.

There were restaurants in the shopping center restaurant area near where they were but decided to take back one from the diner.

They were finished dining, purchasing a dinner for Madeleine, and were in the car set to head back to the lei stand. As they headed back they passed the garden and park where they had just been.

Back at the lei stand Madeleine, who was within hearing distance of the lei venue as well as the songwriter-singers, was getting restless. She expected they would be back and Fred would have the plate lunch for her. It had been a couple of hours since they had left and they were getting into lunchtime.

As they were returning, which was after their eating the dessert of the restaurant's lunch wagon, haupia pie.

Just after they finished they went to Fred's car. He unlocked the car, unlocked the passenger side so Wallace could enter, and were soon driving back to the lei venue site where the numerous gardens were.

After parking the car, they got out, and Fred carrying Madeleine's plate lunch hopped over a curb and walked across a grassy area where some bushes grew to give Madeleine, waiting at the benches near the singer-songwriters, her deluxe mahi-mahi plate still warm.

Fred handed Madeleine the mahi-mahi plate lunch and sat beside her. They were together again.

Fred Langley was seated comfortably next to Madeleine, who also was comfortable, finishing the mahi-mahi plate on her lap. The two scoops of rice and coleslaw on the side were usual. She finished up, and she and Fred went to the lei stand. As they walked, she wondered if Sam and Frank would be playing songs far into the afternoon, sometimes they did, and sometimes they didn't. She was looking forward to browsing the lei stand, maybe Fred would buy her a corsage. The thirty or so yards they walked to it were lined with gardenia bushes, coconut trees were back from the gardenia, and hibiscus. A tour group, who had recently arrived in the islands was there, about six visitors were browsing around the lei stand. Madeleine and Fred stopped short of the lei stand, and enjoyed the landscaping, they were relaxed and listening to the enjoyable music and having eaten an early lunch.

In the distance toward the south was a rainbow. Frank and Sam paused in their playing their ukuleles and faced it. It was distant in front of a rain cloud, which made one think, how does that produce the rainbow that got in front of the cloud? It was by the wind. And a shower was threatening as they finished their song, and again after returning their ukuleles to a finer pitch, they played another song as the rainbow faded part by part.

After the group left the lei stand, which was about a quarter-hour, they were still enjoying the music and the group was like taking their place as they came to the lei stand.

in the distance, Sam and Frank were introducing aloha to the visitors of the tour group, who took seats.

Frank proclaimed, "Aloha."

Sam added, "Aloha."

There were some attentive faces.

Frank and Sam, in unison, proclaimed, "Aloha."

There were a few faint replies of "Aloha".

Frank and Sam played "Valleys, Mountains, and the Ocean". They paused.

A couple of people from the tour group placed dollar bills in the hand-woven coconut frond basket in front of the musicians. As they were listening to the duo's song, the music for a while, they paused, got comfortable in the seats, and relaxed as they finished singing.

Frank and Sam, together, complemented, "Mahalo."

The thank you word was understood and some visitors added to the basket.

Since Frank had stopped playing, and Sam was looking around in the quiet applause that followed the song, a couple, a man and a woman from the group, applauded vigorously, which inspired Sam to start strumming his ukulele again. He quickly strummed out holding a chord and then supported the song rhythm they had just played. It was a slightly slower tempo. Some of the crowd there were pacified by the music. The song, which was a short but slow song, had a tempo that stretched it out, and as the pretty melody gave it a listen-to sound, the deep feeling and complicated chords of it were resonating.

Sam commented, "It sort of reminds you of a native village somewhere."

There was a breeze, and the music shifted to a moderate tempo as Frank and Sam warmed up and played their tunes. The breeze was the trade wind breeze that swept up a little of the odors from the lei stand and some plumeria trees in bloom nearby and the tour group listening to the tune was happy to be there.

Madeleine, who had finished her plate lunch, had walked to the lei stand to see June Nani. And Wallace was there, chatting, but straining to hear the music of Sam and Frank, which was a little faint that day as the breeze went the other way from the lei stand. The tune was a happy tune, and the sound of it was fine, it started some of the tour group wandering around the area, and some members of the group were pausing at tagged bushes and reading the informative paragraph.

The lunch hour passed, and the afternoon came and came toward a close. It was later in the afternoon and June Nani, who was always nearby the lei venue, was thinking it was time for closing for the day. The tour groups had come and gone, and the people who liked to come and hike were there.

Wallace, who had come early before lunchtime, had gone on a hike throughout most of the afternoon. A couple of locals, a man and wife, had come and gone on a hike passing by the lei stand and the singer-songwriters and taken a well-marked trail. The afternoon hike was beckoning June Nani, who was relaxing in a fold-out chair next to her lei stand. She shuttered half of the lei stand and relaxed further. It was mid to late afternoon, and the days were a little shorter, it was past the long days of summer. Her nephew, Mack, was there.

June Nani informed, "I'm going to hike up the fern forest trail and look out toward the town, there's a lookout up there. I won't be long, it's not a long trail."

Mack complied, "OK, I will keep an eye on it.

"Maybe I'll be right back."

"OK."

June Nani got up out of her fold-out chair, and walked to the opposite side of the large parking lot, aiming for the trail. She had found an entrance to it the day before, it was into a much-visited forest reserve, but not much of it to see at the entrance. And she went down the trail over a hill and across another trail opening up to a wide walkway.

It felt good to be out on the hiking trail. As she came back, she saw Mack.

She, also, saw Wallace, who liked to hang out till dusk.

She commented, "Wallace, I don't hike much, but it's more than a reward for me."

Wallace replied, "Come hike with me, June Nani. Maybe not today, but sometime?"

"She replied, "That's OK,"

It was the next day, June Nani had returned from her short hike, and this day had come to open the lei stand. In the distance of the park's parking lot and to the side was a grassy area, the benches were hosting a few fans of the mellow songsters who were in front of them. In the air there, there were wafts of great aromas from plumeria trees nearby, and these were so well appreciated by visitors who came to buy leis, listen to music, and wander around.

There was a nice sound that was played by Frank and Sam, the songwriter-singers knew quite a few.

June Nani had wanted to go on a hike. And she went after a while.

The hike was short but enjoyable, it went along a stream, and the trail by the side of a stream was typical, expected, and often intermittent dropping into the stream or a pool of it.

"Come on, June Nani, let's go hiking?" Wallace had asked.

Wallace went on his own hike, she went on hers.

She was returned from her hike, and she reluctantly agreed to hike a way with Wallace.

June Nani commented, "Okay, but I've got to go home and change some leis, the fresh ones for tomorrow. Then I'll be glad to hike."

She returned from her short hike once, having agreed to hike with Wallace.

"So good to hike with you," Wallace said. "Now, I've got my good friend June Nani to h9ke with. She likes to hike, and likes to have someone to hike with."

"That I do," she added.

After a short hike to overlook the surfing beaches, the shoreline was often crowded with those who rode waves, they rested for a while before returning to the car and going back to the park. They really noted there was a musical happening here.

Hiking enthusiasts were sportive, they usually had backpacks, came early, and were able to stay out hiking for hours. Some that hiked there a lot came to enjoy some of the lookouts.

And then there were some standard songs being played by Frank and Sam. Their music drifted into the environment around the lei stand, and on occasion included guitar accompaniment, as a guest someone had a guitar, and after sitting near to them in the audience got invited to instrumentally accompany. The singer-songwriters paused in between the songs. The faint fading out was listened to as a quiet instrumental refrain was so well accompanying a song. And the performance by someone's guitar enchanted those visitors listening there in a group, they applauded and left money in the coconut frond basket.

There was one song that was going on for a while, it was well presented, first sounding like a chant, perhaps of the Hawaiian chant art. Frank and Sam paused momentarily in the song and chanted a few words over and over and then concluded the song was sort of a folkie song as the audience was remaining.

Someone on the other side of the parking lot was coming back from hiking and got into their car as the song was going on. Maybe they would be driving to a part of the island that was seen by hiking out on a trail to a lookout. There was one car driving around the parking lot twice. It was like the music was going on and the singer-songwriters noticed.

As Frank and Sam played into a couple of their new songwriting songs, they knew it was a side sound to the songs that they usually played, they paused and allowed some of the visitors to return to their departing tour group.

In the distance from the parking lot, to the side of the lei stand, a grassy area had benches, where some mellow songs were being delivered live into the air, it reminded the many visors of some of the great locations they had seen in advertisements; and these were so well appreciated by the songs, the singers, the visitors, and hikers. Hiking enthusiasts were ever among the visitors who took a load off their feet in front of the enjoyable singer-songwriters; before or after hiking. The hike to a lookout was memorable.

There were side sounds from birds, the wind, and hikers. The songs that Frank and Sam played included, maybe a couple of songwriting efforts they knew would enhance the song sound of the area.

It was another day. And midday. The usual group of tourists from a tour was there enjoying the artistry of musicians Frank and Sam.

Frank and Sam introduced their promotional songs, Frank took the volume up a little and added a word.

Frank proclaimed, "Aloha."

Sam added, "Aloha."

Frank continued, "You know, we could play songs somewhere interesting and we'd look around and see the basket placed in front. The hats on heads were pulled snug at evening times, the sunlight in the distance demanding care there.

The song they introduced was a soft promotion with moderate solo accompaniment in parts and went waltzing on and on.

The days marched on, and the seasons sometimes, too. The lei stand was as usual hosted, and now included postcards for remembrance. Mack, Wallace, and June Nani were waiting.

June Nani commented, "There are lots of natural shows for visitors to see in the sunset, in the clouds, in the rainbows, and sometimes, in a volcano. Though most volcanoes around here are extinct, if one wants to, they can go to see the near active ones on the outer isle."

Mack added, "That's exciting, June Nani."

Then days as usual passed. Birds were singing, singer-songwriter duo Frank and Sam were looking at each other getting ready to pluck their instruments. They were looking at each other momentarily as a mutual acknowledgment that this was the way they wanted their melodies set to go. They would do their song "Forest Birds" to start. It was a simple song that they had been happy with for a while. With them, it had been a longer song set, and using this "Forest Birds" song, it would be applauded.

They sang the song and it brought smiles from the audience. A couple of their fans called for more. And as an encore, they were keen to their listeners. As they sang the song a few people added to the audience sitting on nearby park benches. One of the benches was old, but clean.

They played their full set that day. As they did the large, white bird, a cattle egret flew about the lawn and glided to land near the natural alcove where the performance was going on. They played on as a few mynah birds grouped to the side of their staging. Frank, who had arranged the song to allow generous ad-libbing of verses, which with repeating verses could find the song could go on further than they might be expected with a song. As Sam was finishing the ending, playing a ukulele instrumental, Frank was patting his ukulele, a way to fade out with the rhythm after the plucking was all done.

Sam played it well.

After the song there were moments when they could put their instruments away; it was the end of their set, the end of their daytime musical exposure. Sam, who had been playing music for years, and a few hours this day, was feeling expended. He was especially keen on his fingers, he rubbed his fretting hand with his index finger, which gently relaxed it; he had been doing a lot of note-bending in the final songs of the set they had just finished.

Friends of Frank and Sam, who were friends of the lei stand, friends of the gardens, friends of the park, friends of the hiking trails were often with their companions. The couples visited the lei venue nearby from early in the morning, usually getting a good word from lei stand person June Nani, who was also selling them a lei. The park, which often had lunch wagons, was busy, some additional visitors had come as tourists and their tour guides were with them in addition. Frank and Sam were, as usual, hosting the people.

As Frank and Sam hailed from behind the microphones, other musicians, friends of theirs, and acquaintances, who were watching them, who were there to watch and perhaps mimic them, this was among the coconut trees that extended from lining the parking lot, this was from across a way where a small grove of banana trees grew to the side of two breadfruit trees, they seemed to always have some breadfruit on them. This foliage seemed to add security to the place, being respectful.

There was an especially secure feeling with the breadfruit trees, as with regard to the diet a well-cooked breadfruit was sumptuous, usually seasoned with coconut milk and butter, perhaps there is a to-taste to add, but the food seemed to add to the diet. Then, the usual performance by Frank and Sam had its occurrences. They increased their sets of occurrences as people were coming. The talk among the visitors paused.

At the lei stand, regulars were about. Fred Langley and Wallace were talking.

Fred asked, "What is the best place on this island, Wallace? My missus and I think it's best on the south side."

Wallace replied, "Oh, Madeleine. How is she?" He paused, then answered, "Anyway, the south side."

Fred added, "I was telling Madeleine that the island may have developed in a late eruption; millions of years ago."

Wallace asked, "What do you think?"

Fred replied, "Well, that's science. Anyway, the islands formed from volcanic action, and are still forming, from over five million years ago.

"And Madeleine is fine, she thanks you for the corsage."

Wallace added, "You're welcome. I know the chain is situated on a shelf that ever so slowly moves north." He looked around, desperate to have the subject changed.

Fred commented, "Yes, those ferns and Ohia trees like to grow right up out of the lava. Only a few score years previous and vegetation!"

Wallace added, "Even an orchid plant crops up."

Fred continued, "They are nice. There are quite a few nice places there in the Fern Forest."

Wallace replied, "Out there in a Fern Forest home; what a nice part of the island to be at, that is my favorite place, the rains are fine, the altitude is high; there it's a very nice place."

Fred added, "There are guava trees and various native plants, some are planted there."

Wallace added, "Yes, there are orange trees, lemon trees, tangerine trees."

Fred added, "That is my favorite place."

Wallace continued, "Yes, maybe there are groves of grapefruit?"

June Nani was talking to her nephew, Mack, who had come with some white ginger blossoms for her and was tying some strings of flowers up for her.

He mentally noted Wallace and his friends were about. Maybe they would buy some flowers, leis, or some of the other things his aunt had to sell. Wallace was a visitor who usually purchased something to take home to his wife; sometimes, he bought something for his friend, Fred, and Madeleine, Fred's wife. Fred didn't mind, and he had said so.

Mack sometimes would hike to the other side of the fern grotto on to the entrance to a hiking trail that went through a gulch. He might hike with Wallace.

Wallace asked, "Are you coming with me today? I'm going on a short hike down the gulch and up the stream; probably see some o'u birds."

June Nani commented, "The o'u birds are a critically endangered species."

Wallace replied, "I'm still going hiking. You coming, Mack?"

Mack replied, "Oh, I don't think so, Wallace. Maybe my aunt will?" He turned to June Nani, lifting his eyebrows.

She replied, "No, Mack. I am not going hiking today."

There were days when she did; and of those, sometimes Mack tended to the lei stand.

Mack commented, "I remember when all this area here," he waved with his arm, slowly encompassing a semicircle in front where coconut trees, breadfruit trees, plumeria trees, and taro patches were growing, "was from way back."

June Nani added, "It was all ferns."

Wallace knew the way through the fern fields, they went a long way around the mountains toward the mountain's tops. The gulches were covered with them. If one starts at the bottom, perhaps just having hiked up the stream to a not too steep point, just the other side of the fern fields up, it dips into another gulch that falls into the rocky stream at the bottom. That is one hike to go on.

Mack commented, "One place; that's where the thistle berries grow."

The melodies continued coming from Frank and Sam. They were singing about ferns in different situations with different songs. They sang "Fern Forest" and "Fern Forest Blues".

The song was unique, and Frank added, "As we are for the second time around of the song we are singing, we are singing it softer."

"It has a nice introduction," said Sam.

June Nani commented, "If it's not about a Fern Forest residence, they've got the blues for the fern forest ambiance."

The Langleys, who were there, were enjoying the song they had been listening acutely to. Also, there were strange bird songs and some nice weather.

The pleasant ambiance allowed the hiking Wallace to stroll to a position for listening to the singers, who often talked with pleasant ambiance. After a couple of songs, the Langleys strolled there and came back to chat with June Nani, who had had her back to the lei stand. She was rotating around as usual, customers were the norm there.

"Well," Fred Langley announced, "We're taking the fern flower corsage." He looked at June Nani, then Madeleine, and said, "Then we'll be going home."

"OK," Madeleine agreed.

"OK," June Nani replied. And she handed him his usual corsage of a large, cultivated orchid with a tender maidenhair fern on its spindle.

The lei stand, the long-standing premier venue that had always closed its shutters early in the afternoon, but was open. June Nani had managed to have out a few packages of fern and flower corsages. They were for sale as Fred Langley bought two for his wife.

Wallace and Marty had come about to go on separate hikes in the late morning the following day. They were talking to the side of the lei stand. They strolled to where the music was set to be happening.

"My friend, Marty," Wallace said, "you are working a steady job, even if it is on a sailboat, now you have a good chance of staying here. Why don't you stay in a room somewhere?"

Marty replied, "Maybe I will.

"My friend June Nani picks fern flower corsages for me to buy, and I buy them. I come here and go to the hiking area."

Wallace added, "Yes, now that you're off a boat, you can take your time and enjoy the signs and sounds. You may as well."

Marty added, "You know, I have June Nani for a friend, she sells packed fern and flower corsages, leis, and flowers. You know June Nani?"

"Yes, she's selling leis and making corsages. I buy a corsage most of the time when I come here."

June Nani was just lowering the shutters to her venue for the day. She came in front where the two men were talking. She said, "After I'm through work I am pau *hana*, finished with work." Then she commented, "Well, take another moment and listen to Sam and Frank. They have a nice show."

Mack, June Nani's nephew, was listening. He was sometimes a pineapple picker. He stepped closer to where June Nani, Wallace, and Marty were talking.

Marty commented, "So, Wallace; you come from the area where there is work on cars?"

Marty replied, "Some cars are worked on."

Mack commented, "It's good to get a new car."

Marty added, "They're OK."

June Nani came from around the side of the lei venue.

She added, "When are you going to fix my jalopy, Mack? I am glad to see you because my car has a flat. You know? You know how to fix wheels?"

Mack replied, "I know. Sometime."

"Soon!" June Nani added.

Wallace commented, "When we come back to my house, Mack, the guy, I'll let you stay. We know you are a good guy, and we're always glad to see Mack around. It's home." Wallace looked to the side, then continued, "I like Mack because he picks pineapple and works hard in the pineapple fields. He gets the room and the work is good. All we have to have is a little help with the lawn ferns, they need to be weeded and trimmed back." He looked at Mack and added, "You do the work as a truck driver?"

Mack replied, "Ya, I drive a truck sometimes. In the pineapple fields, and delivery work sometimes."

June Nani added, "That's right."

"Yeah, I do some work in the pineapple fields, I also do handyman jobs. I got to live here, too."

Wallace commented, "He was living near where I live when I moved in. He'd like to rent, and live here."

Mack added, "I would really like to live in a fern house in the isles' fern forest."

Wallace added, "That's another island. Big Isle?"

June Nani commented, "There, too."

Mack added, "I live here for now, this is where family is. Next door, there is a young person who regularly goes to work in the fields. I know he picks where I have picked."

June Nani commented, "Mack and his friend travel some."

Wallace asked, "You're picking pineapples too?"

"He was living near there. He'd like to rent," commented Wallace.

Mack remarked, "I would like to live in a fern house on another island."

Wallace commented, "I will note, friend, you are family. Next door to my family, there is a young man who regularly works in the pine fields. Mack, you and this friend could travel a lot. I know you have places to go to, too."

Fred asked, "You have worked in the pineapple fields, too, haven't you, Wallace?"

"Yes," Wallace replied, "I've worked a little here, a little there, it was a long time ago."

"How do you get by now?" Fred asked.

Wallace looked defeated and had time to think.

Mack added, "They teach a person to pick pineap-les in that, when they pick them, they are unbruised fruit, just like as they are growing, they don't want you to break the crown off the pineapple by slamming it on the boom as you walk along. No. When you pick the fruit, you have to carefully twist the crown off, or sometimes push it, maybe putting it on your knee and pushing it if it's a rare multiple crown. Sometimes the crowns are so tight it's hard to get them off. If you take a break you fall behind, so it is good to just twist the crown off. Now, if you take a break with the boom picker truck turning around at the end of a row, there is a moment to break."

Wallace considered picking pineapples again.

Fred asked, "Does it make you more money at night?"

Mack replied, "I make money at night, the pay grade goes up. Afternoon into the night, and I go to work during the day for a few weeks later. Maybe go to another island."

"Sure, sounds good," Wallace commented.

"It's good with housing," Mack added.

Fred and Wallace, being tired, were about to go to their homes this evening.

Fred commented, "I could be going to a hula luau with Madeleine this week. Do you want to come?"

Wallace replied, "I've been to a hula luau recently, so I don't think so."

Frank and Sam were through playing their songs for a while and listened in.

Mack commented, "I like to live in a fern house. When I pick pineapple, I walk across the fields on my day off. We go to the beach and swim."

Sam commented, "We play ukuleles."

Mack added, "When we come back to the ferns, the fern house is waiting."

Frank added, "When we do our outer island gig, we play for a tour group here and there, then we come back and enjoy playing for this group around here."

"Mack added, "Well, I'll come back, too." He looked at June Nani, and commented, "So I come home to my room from the fern home, it's where I rent a room. I hike some, and after I do some other jobs, I polish June Nani's car, I mow their lawn, I get one room."

Frank added, "You're still going to live in the fern house?"

Mack replied, "Yes, I am still there."

Wallace added, "Good for you, Mack. Two homes."

June Nani commented, "OK, Mack, you are accepting my offer for work, you can do some outside the house work, take care of the yard."

Sam and Frank were about ready to go but decided there was time to do one more song."

Frank commented, "Fern house, fern home, that's what the song says."

There was a light breeze blowing in this early evening, an unusual breeze, which wasn't with the standard ambiance, which was with bird songs and bird calls.

Sam commented, "We play "Fern Forest", we can play "Pineapple Fields".

The song they played, "Fern Forest" ended and the coterie of folks were standing outside of the park benches for a while. There was a little applause as Frank and Sam were gracious, bowing and smiling.

"It has been our pleasure," Frank added.

Sam added, "Thank you for allowing us to do these songs. We had a great time."

Frank stood up from the folding chair where he had been playing the ukulele and singing. He stepped to the other side of Sam, cocked his head sideways so he could hear Sam, who was putting away his ukulele in a nice, hardwood case, and sighed.

Sam lightly patted the case and it sounded like a drum, he stood and did a hula move, he had a feel for hula, and for about a minute he was animated, rotating his hips around and around.

Frank commented, "We could go on with our home land sound, Sam, but."

Sam added, "Not now, Frank, it's late and we're headed home."

Wallace and the rest were watching them, they noticed this and looked back at Wallace, who was standing next to Mack.

Mack walked up to Frank, Sam was standing by and closely watching, the rhythm just played was still going through his mind and he was bouncing his head to a beat and snapping his fingers, keeping his bagged ukulele close to his body.

Mack smiled and commented, "Next time you guys play here, play something with a little more feeling? OK?"

Frank replied, "OK, we got a feeling song.

As this was late in the day, a visitor was coming out of a nearby trail entrance. These people had been out in the first reserve from early in the day, they went right to their car, got in and went home.

It had been a while and Sam and Frank were conferring on playing another song.

Sam asked, "Maybe we ought to redo some love songs? We can play our songs."

Frank replied "It's OK, Sam. This is the end of the day."

Marty was there,

He commented, "Even out there on that trail we were hiking today, it seemed we could hear you playing your songs, but as the trail went ;around with the curvature of the gulch, on the side of the stream, it faded out and we couldn't hear it. We kept walking.

Sam added, "One more song. We're always good for one more song. But we thank you for allowing us to enjoy the song."

Frank added, "One more song, mahalo very much, mahalo."

Frank and Sam quickly took their ukuleles out and played singing sweetly, "Fern Forest Blues".

It was early evening twilight as Frank and Sam played their song. Somewhat a last song, "Fern Forest Blues" was allowing their ad lib.

Frank commented, "This was a song of our visit to the fern forest."

They finished, once again putting their instruments in their cases, bowing out, they decided it was too late to play more and were headed to their home.

June Nani commented, "No, certainly not."

Marty asked, "Can you possibly sing another of your songs?"

June added, "No? Certainly?"

Sam added, "Heavenly flowers." It was a musical comment, and for a while the night twilight was lingering and saying goodbye was like it was yesterday.

Marty excused himself, "Goodbye,"

He was saying because he was going to work, quick to leave, excusing himself. The Langleys lingered a while, enjoying the cool breeze this evening. The Langleys drove to a restaurant for a mahi mahi plate dinner. As the moderate breeze blew, they eventually cruised to their home a few blocks away.

June was about the last to leave, and she sang, "Heavenly Flowers". The song was with a chord, and since most of the regulars had left, was heading home.

Wallace commented, "The fern house is a nice place to go to, from there you can see, like a vacation, all the way to the sea, there's where rain floats in on the breeze, and you can see the distant horizon ocean."

June Nani added, "There goes the Langleys, every day, one mahi mahi plate. And they're family."

Wallace added, "There are lookouts for you, if you go the beach side trail."

Wallace has swam at the bottom of a waterfall in a pool, this was a day to remember. He had viewed the precipice to the sea as evening clouds drifted onto and over the mountain tops.

Since the last tourist group had left and June Nani had shuttered and locked the lei stand, packing away some leis and flowers for the next day, Wallace was driving to his nice house, where his wife was expecting him. He drove by a beach and into his driveway.

Marty, who had sailed to the outer islands, was on a boat sailing to some South Sea islands. But he would be back.

Mr. Thwarton, the lawyer, who had come again and taken a few green coconuts, was looking forward to his home, a rural residence on the other side of the island. There, he had a pickaxe to stick in the ground.

He slammed the pickaxe into the ground and took one of the coconuts to husk. He slammed its side onto the pointed side of the pickaxe, pushed down, and pulled off the fibrous husk. He, then, took a pocket knife and poked at the soft socket of the coconut, one of the three eyes was sort, and quickly poured out the liquid elixir and enjoyed the blessing that was especially good. It was a treat worth the wait.

Even June Nani had a green coconut to take home this evening, and her husband knew right where to stick the pick. They shared the drink of coconut juice, as well as the pulp that came with it.

There were tourists returning to their home, some had been asked to keep their hand-woven ti plant leis given to them so when they were on the plane home, they could remember the visit.

Sam and Frank were included in a small nightclub at a hotel. They were well liked by local customers, who came just to see them, as well as well promoted to touring groups. If they had a hall there would be many people attending.

They knew other performers were ahead of them, since they usually played at the park where the lei stand was, they were having a few showroom gigs. There were newcomers often looking for a spot to play.

Wallace and his adventures to streams, which set him a little into the wilds there, enjoyed the drink of an artesian water occasionally that fed some stream that he walked up. He continued with his friends Fred Langley and others on trails from openings into the forest reserves.

Mack, an experienced body surfer, enjoyed his days off going to the Windward side and visiting the treasured body surfing of Makapuu. This was on his days off, when the music was happening again.

As Sam and Frank finished a last song in the evening, gifts and change from the crowd included a fill of the ukulele cases, they found herbal tea bags.

"Hibiscus," Sam exclaimed. "I'll have this hibiscus tea tonight." He put the teabag in his bag and counted out the dollars in small bills and change that had accumulated.

Frank commented, "We did pretty good today?"

Sam replied "Yes, we did. And there were two tea bags. Here's one for you."

Frank took the herbal tea bag and put it in his pocket.

"Thanks," he replied.

As he was finishing putting up the ukulele, he hummed a song.

Sam treasured his old ukulele, an instrument that had been repaired.

The next day, Wallace went to some roadside beach park, where there were a few papaya trees growing free and wild. He picked two ripe ones, one for a later papaya break, and then, one to take home to his wife, Anita. He and they enjoyed the small, ripe papaya from the low tree, and he looked off the beachside at the roadside park site as surf was splashing up on a rock pile.

Many were the visitors who had stopped by the same site and were then returning by air, to where their views were remembered from informative brochures from their hotels' lobby stands. There were views of the island skies and beach lookout sites.

While many local people were busy with jobs, some were in the evening dedicated to enjoying the shows, shows like Frank and Sams were going on with a real local flair.

While Sam and Frank had played some of their blues, and other duos and groups performed regularly, there were visitors from the mainland regularly keeping a show date.

Wallace, who had been lat hiking this one recent evening, came back finally wandering to his car in the dusk parked at a well paved parking lot, but past the enjoyment of late twilight, and admired the light from the metropolis he lived in, there were many glows in the sky as he signed and pulled out of the parking lot and went home

Frank and Sam, who had played a last song, a blues song pattern, were somewhat relaxed as they had gazed toward the sunset and upwards spotting unblinking stars. Planets probably. A couple such night lights would be sinking in their own time.

As the sunset had grown into a panorama of orange from sunlight reflecting the distant, low cloud bank, things were happening. Sam and Frank, who had been through singing and driven to their home, an apartment building on the edge of town, were passing on clubbing that night.

The distant stars were starting to come out, the half moon came out with the early twilight.

www.ingramcontent.com/pod-product-compliance
Lightning Source LLC
Chambersburg PA
CBHW070354310726
48977CB00002B/433